A KING FOR A QUIET

BY

N.M. HALL

The disappearance of the Reverend Jason Bell, Rector of Bereston, Tarnswell, whose car is found abandoned on St. Eldon's Cliffs in May, two thousand and fourteen, coincides with the funeral and burial of the Archdeacon of Wydebridge, the Venerable Martin Hind.

Several months later the Bishop of Tarnswell asks Martin's widow, the Reverend Dora Hind, to take Sunday services at Bereston while the Diocese waits for definite news. Dora agrees, feeling that her late husband would have wanted her to do this.

Having taken up her duties, Dora finds herself conducting her own private investigation into Jason's disappearance. As she builds her theory about what may have happened, so she reflects upon her own loss, and her life without Martin.

Some characters in this story also appear in my novel 'Cranmer's Children'.

I

On Friday May the sixteenth, in the year two thousand and fourteen, I awoke in the small hours. I got up and looked out of the bedroom window and across the village street towards the little parish church of St. Clement, in the village of Chedd. It was still dark, so I put on my dressing gown and went downstairs as quietly as possible and made myself a cup of tea in the kitchen. It had taken me two hours to get to sleep that night and I was not at all surprised to have woken so early.

When it was light outside I got dressed and took the key to the church from the hook in the kitchen cupboard. I was at that time still licensed as a non-stipendiary assistant priest in the Parish of Chedd and two neighbouring village churches. Now I took the key along with my house keys, opened the front door of the Old Rectory, and closed it quietly behind me. I set out across the deserted road and through the churchyard and let myself into the church.

St. Clement's Chedd is one of my favourite churches: it is historic but quite plain with wooden floors and beams and clean lime-washed plaster. Between the altar, which was dressed in white with a single votive lamp burning, and the stand of white lilies below the chancel step, stood the trestles bearing my husband's coffin, on the top of which lay his white ordination stole. Because he was a priest the coffin was placed with his head towards the altar.

In the silence of that church, where we had so often worshipped or sat quietly together, I spoke to my husband. 'Later this morning,' I told him, 'You will be carried to Tarnswell Cathedral, where your family and hundreds of friends and colleagues and past parishioners will gather to be with you. For now, I have this time to be alone with you, to tell you how much I have loved you, and always will; how much I miss you, how happy my life has been with you. After the Cathedral service, with your family and your closest friends, I will make the journey with you to Tarnswell Highfields Churchyard where your first wife Elizabeth lies buried, and, as you wished you will be interred with her.'

I told him that I would do my very best to live on with the memory of his love and the hope of our faith to comfort me in the difficult times, and to continue to be a friend to his children and their families. Then I kissed his coffin, placed my hand gently upon it and said, 'I love you, Martin. Christ is Risen.'

I left the church, locking it behind me, and made my way back to the Old Rectory where two of Martin's three children and their families were waking.

II

As I would later discover, a priest called Jason Bell, Rector of St. Thomas, Bereston, in the Diocese of Tarnswell, drove his car in the small hours of that same morning to a layby on St. Eldon's Cliffs, locked it, and tucked the keys behind the nearside front wheel. The arrival of the car was witnessed by the owner of the St. Eldon Hotel, who, having woken early and used the bathroom, looked out of the window half asleep and saw the car drive up and stop; he did not recognise it, he turned away and returned to bed.

It was soon reported that Jason Bell had disappeared.

III

Before moving to Bereston in two thousand and twelve, Jason Bell had served for seventeen years as the vicar of another Parish in the Diocese, in whose architecturally significant Georgian church he had overseen an extensive restoration and reordering project. At the age of fifty-two he had agreed with the Bishop that it was time to move on to another post and he was encouraged to apply for St. Thomas', Bereston, which lay about two miles from the centre of the City of Tarnswell and had once been the parish church of a self-contained village. Norman in origin, St. Thomas' was considered to be a very fine largely medieval building in an extensive churchyard that was still open for parish burials.

The nine parishes in and around the City of Tarnswell – some of them already embracing more than one parish church - were at that time in the process of becoming one single parish with several 'Local Worshipping Communities', each with its own 'Local Priest'. It was, therefore, a time of significant change.

The people of Bereston were proud of their village and its church; many of them considered themselves residents of Bereston rather than Tarnswell, and they did not welcome this development; however, assurances had been given that they would always have their own Rector, although they would be required to get used to his new, and to some unsatisfactory, title of 'Local Priest'. The Diocese favoured this term in this kind of project because it identified all those who, stipendiary or non-stipendiary or living free in a vicarage in exchange for Sunday worship and some weekday duties, were functioning in a particular parish as its named priest. Jason was aware when he took up his post in two thousand and twelve that there were mixed feelings about these new arrangements, but that it was his job to accommodate the change and make it work.

By two thousand and fourteen Jason was well established in Bereston and widely respected, but the new arrangement involved a lot of additional meetings. Jason was a single man, he had a great love of beautiful buildings and objects, and he had the reputation of being a dedicated priest. Both his parents were dead; he had made no secret of the fact that they had adopted him. He had no brothers or sisters. He had put himself forward for selection for the Anglican ministry after university at the age of twenty-four, but he had been told to get more experience in the world of work; he had worked for a charity for the next five years but he had never contemplated any other vocation, and he was eventually accepted for ordination training. His greatest friend and spiritual director was an older priest, Father Hilton Denyer, who had been the vicar of the parish where Jason served his title or first curate's post. Father Denyer had died in Jason's first year at Bereston, and the following month in the Bereston Parish Magazine Jason had written of his deep appreciation of Father Denyer's example and guidance to himself and to the many curates he had trained and in whom he had instilled high standards of ministry.

In two thousand and fourteen, Easter Sunday fell on April the twentieth. Easter is one of the two great festivals of the Christian year, and Holy Week and Easter are liturgically demanding, so It is normal for clergy to take time off in Easter week. It so happened however, that Jason had found himself with five funerals, spread over the four working days. The last one fell on the Friday, which was Jason's day off. The Friday before had been Good Friday when of course he had been at work, conducting several services. He could have delegated that last funeral at least, but he thought that he should, as parish priest, officiate at them all. In the event, however, he forgot about it. He went out for the day, and when he came back there was a message on his phone from the undertakers; when he looked at his mobile which he kept on silent on his day off, he saw that there were messages there too.

The funeral in question was at Tarnswell Cemetery chapel, and it was straightforward, by which I mean, from my own experience, that it was uncomplicated. The deceased was a widowed man who had lived in Jason's parish, but had not attended the church. He had no children but his nephew, who lived some distance away, made the arrangements by telephone and email. There were no hymns, it was to be the minimal service followed immediately by his burial in the grave in the cemetery already occupied by his late wife, and the nephew would give the 'eulogy'.

When Jason did not appear, and his landline and mobile phone both went to voicemail, the undertaker asked the priest who had taken the previous service, and who was fortunately still standing by that graveside with the mourners, to conduct this funeral, which, graciously, he agreed to do. So the funeral took place more or less on time, and in a style that accorded with the family's wishes, and since none of the mourners knew Jason, most seemed satisfied with the priest they had.

But shortly afterwards the nephew's wife contacted the *Tarnswell Times*, the local paper, which ran a fairly discreet story the following Thursday, not wanting to alienate Jason, who always kept them well-informed about parish life. Unfortunately, a sharp-eyed journalist from a national tabloid newspaper picked the story up and produced a larger item with a photograph of Bereston Church – despite the fact that the funeral did not take place there - and another of the nephew's wife looking dismayed, under the headline: *'Vicar's No-Show At Funeral'*.

Jason, mortified by his mistake, had already contacted the nephew and the undertakers, and the priest who officiated, with sincere apologies. The Area Dean and the Archdeacon of Cartlington, who was doing my late husband's work, contacted Jason and told him to hang in, that it would all blow over. The Bishop of Tarnswell wrote to the family and made a statement to the local paper affirming Jason's qualities as a priest and pastor and giving some idea of the pressures that he had been under at that time. The parish stood firmly by him.

But on that Friday in May as I woke so early, and looked out of the window of the Old Rectory towards Chedd Parish Church where Martin's coffin lay, Jason Bell's car arrived at St. Eldon's Cliffs, and he disappeared.

IV

I married Martin Hind on Easter Monday in the year two-thousand at St. Mark's Church, Wydebridge Green, where I was priest in charge. The then Bishop of Tarnswell, the Right Reverend Giles Blane, officiated. I had already submitted my resignation, and I had led the Holy Week and Easter Services there for the last time. My resignation allowed the parish to be taken under the wing of the Vicar of the Parish of St. Cosmas and St. Alban, Wydebridge, as part of the Wydebridge Deanery Plan to reduce the numbers of stipendiary clergy.

At that time Martin had been Archdeacon of Wydebridge for three years; his responsibilities covered half of the Diocese of Tarnswell, about a hundred and fifty parishes and the deaneries to which they belonged. He worked very hard, spending a lot of time travelling, dealing with legal and ministerial matters, attending or hosting meetings, officiating at services, and sometimes getting involved in quite difficult situations. Martin had been ordained in his twenties and while I think he had most enjoyed being a parish priest, he was popular and effective as Archdeacon. His first wife, Elizabeth, had died in a car accident just a few weeks after he took up the post, which had made his first year much more difficult; Elizabeth's death also took any remaining ambition away; he served as Archdeacon of Wydebridge for seventeen years, until he died.

I had known Martin professionally since nineteen ninety-four, for he had been a parish priest and also Area Dean of Wydebridge before being appointed Archdeacon. Our relationship began a year after Elizabeth died. It was not entirely smooth: he was still working through his grief. Eventually, however, we seemed to find the right path, and we married.

Martin and Elizabeth had three children, all in their twenties by the time I married him. The eldest, Sarah, bore a close physical resemblance to her mother. She was a single parent living at the Old Rectory with her daughter Beth. Abigail was more like Martin, with the same light brown hair and gentle manner. She studied medicine and went into medical research; she eventually married a general practitioner whom she had met at university, and they had three children.

Jamie was Martin and Elizabeth's youngest child. He studied computer graphics and went to work for a small firm on the outskirts of London, commuting every day by car and train. He fell in love with a woman for whom he did some work and moved into her expensive flat. She was always polite but both Martin and I felt that she tolerated rather than welcomed Jamie's family. One day he rang to ask if he could come back to live at the Old Rectory for a while. He arrived looking depressed and tired. We gave him space and eventually he told us that his partner had found someone else. He had very little money because he had spent everything helping to maintain the flat and their costly standard of living. He began commuting again and gradually he took up his old life; he had been a teenager when the family moved to Chedd and he had many friends there and in Wydebridge. One evening he was invited to make up a foursome, and to Jamie's surprise he knew the unattached woman already, she had been his girlfriend some years before.

We had noticed that Jamie seemed his old self again, easy-going and happy. One day he asked if he could bring his girlfriend home. I cooked a special meal and he went to fetch her. He introduced her as 'Zoe'; she was petite, pretty, with bobbed fair hair. Martin shook her hand, asked that her name be repeated and stared at her and said:

'Are you… the Zoe who came to church with us that Christmas?' Zoe and Jamie both laughed, 'Yes,' she said, 'That's me.'

So I heard the story of how, that first sad Christmas after Elizabeth's death, Zoe, then only seventeen, and Jamie's girlfriend, had asked if she could go to a midnight service at Farfields Parish Church which Martin was taking and his children had all agreed to attend. At that time Zoe had favoured a rather exotic style of dress and heavy kohl eye make-up, and she remembered how Martin had tried to cover his surprise when she had told him that she was a 'sort of Buddhist'.

'Actually, you were a great inspiration to me,' said Martin as we all ate together, 'You gave me a clue for my key address at the Diocesan Conference.'

'Really?' she said, rather pleased.

'Yes. You were so interested in the service, even though you said you had only been to church with your school.'

'That's right,' Zoe said, 'And I didn't think people like me were allowed to go to church services, people who didn't belong.'

'That's just it,' Martin said, looking seriously at her; 'You *did* belong, everyone belongs. The Church is for everyone.'

I could see Jamie smiling, and I knew he was thinking, 'Here comes another sermon.' But Martin and Zoe got on well and he was very happy when she and Jamie married;

in fact he married them himself at Chedd, with the Vicar's permission. Zoe wore a beautiful lace dress, sparkling with tiny gems. By that time they had managed to get a mortgage on a small new flat in Wydebridge; they have one son, now at primary school.

Thinking about Zoe, I want to go back to that happy evening. I want to be there again with the man I loved: the gentle, straightforward priest for whom the Church had always been a home, a substitute for the father who deserted his mother when she developed multiple sclerosis, and left her and her son in the proud poverty of those years after the second world war, when nothing was cheap and only a section of the population really had it so good. People these days perhaps do not realise that the Church still makes a great difference in some people's lives. After all, the Church's message is the possibility of hope, change and a different future. With a mother struggling with poverty and ill-health, and no father, Martin might have become a very different person: in the event, at nine years old, he found the Church, and the Church changed everything for him.

Martin died at home in Chedd Old Rectory on Easter Sunday. He had never smoked in his life, but as a young curate serving in a town called Amerton he had cycled in and out of traffic belching out high-octane emissions. Years later that would bring on the cancer from which he died, after a two-year struggle, at the age of sixty-five. Thanks to his share of the money inherited by Elizabeth from her family, we were able to afford a male nurse in the final weeks, to care for him at home.

Towards the end he began to think that I was Elizabeth. The nurse said kindly, 'Don't worry, that sometimes happens.' But eventually I went and got the photo of Martin and Elizabeth taken on a holiday in the Cotswolds and I put it on the table near the special bed and I said, 'There's Elizabeth.' He looked at her and smiled slightly, and said, 'Yes, Elizabeth.' Then I took his hand and I held it to the side of my face and I said, very gently, 'I'm Dora.' He looked at me and he smiled at me, and he said, 'Yes, Dora.'

He mostly slept through Good Friday and Holy Saturday and woke very briefly early on Easter Sunday. The local Vicar came round after the morning services, anointed Martin and said some beautiful prayers, and the room was full of Easter flowers. I said, 'Christ is risen' and 'I love you.' The children were there, taking their turn to sit with their father and the nurse and me. He slipped away just after two o'clock.

Christ is risen.

V

The Bishop of Tarnswell came to see me five months later, in September.

I had by that time vacated the Old Rectory at Chedd, which would be required for the next Archdeacon, and I was living in Tarnswell and worshipping at the eight o'clock service at the Cathedral. I had surrendered my licence to serve at Chedd in exchange for permission to officiate in the Diocese where needed, but I had not taken a service since almost a year before my husband died. Although the Cathedral had complex memories for me because I had attended so many services there supporting Martin, I had also been ordained deacon and priest there, and it was my spiritual home. Its gothic walls were lined with memorials to the dead, some elaborately carved with weeping figures: it comprehended my grief.

Between us, Martin and I had already bought a small townhouse in Tarnswell; we had planned to live there when he retired. I had given up full-time stipendiary ministry when I got married at the age of forty-two, but I had savings and my widowed father died four years later leaving me – his only child - his bungalow and the greater part of his money. Although Martin often functioned at the Cathedral, he had never actually lived or served in a parish in the City of Tarnswell, and nor had I, so it was possible for us to retire there. In the event, Martin had become ill at sixty-three, two years before the age at which he had hoped to retire, and by his own wish he struggled on for those two more years until the last few months, and then he died.

I was fortunate to be able to move so easily. I did not hurry, the children needed time to visit the Old Rectory, their old home, and say goodbye to it; but once the immediate period of loss was past and the funeral over, I found myself yearning to leave that lovely greystone building, for like all the houses I had lived in since I entered the church's ministry it was not mine; the person whose life and role had made it my home was gone.

VI

So I was settled in the City of Tarnswell when Bishop Robert, who had succeeded Giles Blane as Bishop of Tarnswell five years before, came to see me about Bereston. He was a very tall man and he seemed to fill the little sitting room. He had a cup of coffee and several biscuits and asked me how I was, and he asked after Martin's family. When we had covered these matters, he looked at me and I knew that he wanted something from me.

'Dora,' he said, 'I have come with a request, for you to think over. There is a situation in a Parish and we have to consider how to go forward. I have a plan A, and that concerns *you*; there is also a plan B and a plan C, but I wanted to ask you first. I want you to hear me out and ask any questions, and then take your time to decide whether you feel it's right for you. I don't need to know today.'

'Fair enough,' I said, 'Thank you for that.'

Robert put his mug down and leaned back slightly in his chair. 'It's about the Parish of Bereston, here in Tarnswell. You will, I am sure, know about the disappearance of the Rector – Local Priest as we call them now – Jason Bell?'

'I did hear about it,' I said, 'But with everything that was happening at that time…'

'Of course,' he said. 'And everyone thought Jason would come back.'

'But… he hasn't.'

'No. And, as they say, with the passing of time, that seems less and less likely. It's been nearly five months now. He left everything in the house: his wallet, his phone. His bank account hasn't been touched. No-one has heard anything from him. But without a body…'

I said, 'Did I hear that his car was found on St. Eldon's Cliffs?'

'Yes, in a layby opposite the hotel. Eldon is, what, about five miles from here, and the cliffs a mile or so further? They found the keys under the car. Now people do go there when they… well, we help fund the chaplain who drives about, keeps an eye on things, and I understand there have been occasions when bodies have not been found or only found much later on. We can't rule out the fact that Jason may have taken his life in that way. I gather that chap at the hotel feels quite bad about it, because he saw the car arrive but he was half asleep, and he went back to bed. Well, that's not his fault.'

We sat in a proper silence for a moment; then the Bishop said, 'There was no note, no message, no warning of any kind. The police have said that they are not aware of anything... well, you know what I mean. They have searched his computer and his phone and mobile records and gone through his letters and papers and found nothing - apart from this wretched business about the funeral.'

I did hear something about a funeral.' I was thinking of the strange weeks after Martin died, in which I seemed always to be looking into the distance, seeing nothing. If Martin had been alive and well, he would have known about Jason's disappearance and he would have been very worried about him. But he was dead and I had been coming to terms with my own grief and supporting his family in theirs, and not paying very much attention to anything else.

I can't believe it was just that,' said Robert, with some passion. 'I mean, we made it clear, the staff, that we stood by him; it was a human error and it would have blown over. There was no real harm done, the funeral took place after all, and I gather the nephew was giving the address so Jason would only have been taking the liturgy and the other priest did that very well, considering. *Why* did that woman have to make such a fuss? Mind you, I expect she wishes she hadn't, now.'

Yes,' I said, 'I'm sure she does. When people live alone, like Jason, with no-one at home to share their problems, it must be harder.' I had lived alone for many years before I married Martin, and I knew.

'Indeed, and Jason was very much a single man. He liked his own space. The Rectory is beautifully decorated and furnished, and he has some valuable possessions, we've had to put a lot of stuff in store, to keep it safe. The churchwardens have emptied the fridge-freezer and turned it off, and disposed of perishable food – it's quite a task, you know, but we can't do more than that, because until we know… Anyway, that brings me to plan A.'

'Of course.' I said.

'Well, until Jason returns or contacts us or we know what has happened, we can't do anything. I mean, not for a while. There is a legal period of course…. The churchwardens are doing a great job and the Area Dean and local retired clergy are giving sterling support. But it's not like an interregnum, a vacancy; I feel that they need *someone* – someone just to take most of the Sunday Parish Eucharists, to be their priest, their point of spiritual reference. Now of course the Area Dean could be that but you know what's happening in Tarnswell, we're moving towards this single parish model, there's already one vacancy and the Area Dean's got a lot of work to do. Bereston is a key player of course and the churchwardens are being as helpful as they can, but they need *someone*…'

'I think I know what you mean. Some sort of continuity on Sundays?'

He said, 'I knew you would understand – but of course, that does not mean that it has to be *you*. It was just that I thought of you. And you know, my predecessor's wife thought of you too.'

'Philippa?'

'Yes, they were up recently for the dedication of the new window in the Cathedral. They stayed with us, actually. We were talking about Jason, and Giles was very sad about it. I said that I was thinking of finding someone and Philippa said, immediately, "What about Dora Hind?" Giles said, "Do you think so? Surely she needs time to grieve." And she said. "Well, ask her. She can only say no." So here I am, to ask you.'

I smiled. The last time I had seen the Blanes was at Martin's funeral, at which Giles, retired and living in Somerset, had given the address. At one point he had struggled to go on, but he had also shared stories that made us laugh, which we needed.

Long before they retired, Philippa had been helpful to me in one particular matter. Martin and I did not have children. He had told me before we married that he had done what some responsible men do after their last child is born; he told me that he would have that procedure reversed if I wanted. But I was in my forties, and a test showed that my fertility was low; I could have medication, accepting that there were additional risks in bearing a child at that age. I struggled for a while, knowing that there was probably only a very small window of opportunity; I had known people of my age who had been trying for years to conceive and it was a complex, dominating process. When Philippa, as was her way, asked me directly if I hoped to have children I confided in her and that helped me to decide. I am very fond of my step-grandchildren, especially Beth who was nearly two when we married; I decided to leave things as they were.

Now I learned that Philippa had recommended me to Bishop Robert. I said, 'Can you just clarify exactly what you want this priest to do?'

'Ah,' he said, and I could see that he was glad that I had asked the question. 'As you know Dora, a parish priest has many roles; Jason's roles are being taken on by various people. This isn't about baptisms and weddings and funerals and the Parochial

Church Council – I don't think you need that. It's about the main Sunday Eucharist. It is, as you say, about continuity. All I ask is that you become the most regular officiant at that service, and the odd early morning or mid-week one too if you wish. I ask you because I know you lead worship well and I also think that you preach well, you make people think, and that is what Jason did. I don't want the main act of Sunday worship to suffer from well-intentioned but... well... shall we say, less imaginative sermons? If thoughtful and intelligent preaching is part of the ethos of Bereston, then we should do our best to maintain it.'

I was touched by Robert's words, but I knew that they were true. It would be a commitment, but not an arduous one. At this time of personal grief I did not feel equal to entering into others' sorrow at funerals or their happiness at weddings and baptisms, but since my ordination to the priesthood in nineteen ninety-four, the Eucharist had been the liturgical focus of my ministry, the point at which the people came together to receive Christ both in my interpretation of the word and in the bread and wine consecrated at my hands. Since I left Wydebridge Green and until about a year before Martin's death I had served on various Diocesan committees and taken services in several churches across the Diocese, and I had regularly presided at the first Sunday Eucharist every month at Chedd. Now everything had stopped. The thought of taking a service most Sundays at Bereston seemed a helpful and not a difficult task, the next, if temporary, stage of my ministry and of my life without Martin.

'I guess Bereston is quite a short drive from here?' said Robert.

'Oh yes, and the ring road is not so busy on Sundays.'

I told Robert that I would think and pray about his request and we agreed that I would email him by the end of the week to give him my decision.

VII

The following day, I drove to Bereston.

Martin and I had often walked on St. Eldon's Cliffs, and we usually drove through Bereston on the way. The first time I had remarked how pretty it was and how much still like a village, despite its being part of the city. A narrowing road crossed railway lines and led to what was in effect a village green bordered by some beautiful and historic houses. Bereston Church stood to the right of the green, laid back within its churchyard. It was a fine English church with a tower and two side aisles that gave it, I thought, rather the look of a crouching cat. The churchyard was surrounded by neat black railings. As we drove past I had noticed the old brick wall abutting the railings on the boundary of the churchyard. We drove some distance alongside the wall before it snaked away to the right where I glimpsed new houses under construction.

The website had told me that Bereston Church was open to visitors every weekday morning from ten until twelve.

I parked my car in an unrestricted side road, and walked back to the church. There was a gate to the path that was wide enough for a vehicle, but kept wisely locked, with a smaller, open gate for pedestrian access. Beside the gates stood a noticeboard painted dark blue with the Tarnswell Diocesan heraldic shield and, in gold paint, the words: 'The Parish of St. Thomas, (Church of England), Bereston. Rector: The Reverend Jason Bell'. Beneath in clear lettering there was general information, website details and phone numbers. It was as I looked at that board that I suddenly *felt* the reality of Jason's disappearance, and began to wonder what had happened to him.

I walked through the churchyard to the church in the pleasant September sun. I could see the Rectory ahead through the trees that bordered the east end of the churchyard and I wondered whether it had been sensible to build it there, so that the Rectory family and any visitors had to walk or drive through a churchyard to reach it. There would be an old Rectory somewhere, perhaps one of those fine buildings on the village green. The replacement was merely functional with no architectural merit; if it had been built ten years later, conservation sensibilities would have insisted on something more in harmony with its environment; even from where I was walking it was obvious that the square metal-framed windows should by now have been replaced. What did Jason, who loved beautiful old buildings, think of that?

I turned left into the porch beside the tower; like the church it was built of stone, with a wooden bench running along both sides. The walls were fitted with neat and colourful display boards: Jason's laminated photograph was pinned to one of them; I looked at his round bald head, his smiling face. Underneath was another laminated notice with the words: *'We are grateful to the visiting clergy who are currently officiating at our services.'* Very well put, I thought; no need to try to explain the inexplicable.

Within the church an elderly man welcomed me and handed me a leaflet. He offered to show me round but I thanked him and said that I would be happy to use the information he had given me. It was a glossy, well-produced short guide with coloured pictures and a plan showing the different eras in which St. Thomas' Church had been built and developed. That it originated in Norman times was evident from the rounded, decorated arch between the nave and the chancel. The church was light and airy, for the walls were plastered and clean and the pews were a lighter colour than some and fitted with blue velvet padded runners to make them more comfortable. The north aisle was a pleasant space furnished with wooden chairs with upholstered blue seats and backs, and I saw several memorials on the north wall, with a small gothic door to the left of them. I enjoy church memorials and I saw that all these were dedicated to members of a family called Belinger, of Bereston Hall; the last of them, commemorating Mary Belinger, had been added in nineteen-sixty, when she died at the sadly early age of nineteen. Under her details were the words: *'Grant her safe lodging, a holy rest, and peace at the last'*.

The largest of the memorials was dedicated to Second Lieutenant James Belinger, described as having been *'lost at the Battle of Loos'* in September nineteen-fifteen at the age of twenty-three. It was a fine memorial with his regimental badge in full colour and gold lettering; it paid tribute to his many qualities and concluded with the words: *'He has gone to be with his fathers'*. I presumed that 'fathers' meant 'forefathers', referring to the Belingers going centuries back who had occupied Bereston Hall; the oldest of their memorials was a man and a woman kneeling, facing each other, wearing black clothes and elaborate ruffs, with smaller figures of a man and a woman, presumably their children, alongside, and, sadly, the little upright figure of a swaddled baby. Some of the inscription was in Latin. Another memorial dated from the eighteenth century and took the form of an urn half-hidden by a draped cloth. Apart from the memorial to James Belinger, the later memorials were plain marble tablets with black lettering.

The organ console was in the nave beside the south aisle; the aisle itself contained two vestries, the outer of which housed the structure supporting the organ pipes; the general light airiness of the building was enhanced by the outer vestry door which, unusually, was made of fumed glass etched, to my surprise, with the most beautiful images of birds and flowers in spring; a flourishing swirl of writing proclaimed that the door was dedicated to the memory of Alina Harris, a *'beloved child'* who had died at the age of fourteen: *'She loved the beauty of nature'*.

Loss and sorrow were all around me, and I carried them too. I was alone; my husband was dead and, by my own decision, I had no children. Then I shook off self-pity. Compared to many, I had so much: enough money, a home, a purpose, a country some longed to live in, and Martin's family. I had also known his love. Death had taken him away from me, but it could not take the memory of his love.

I turned now to the chancel and the sanctuary with its victorian carved reredos of the Last Supper on the east wall. The leaflet explained that the original great east window above it had been blown out by a stray bomb in the war and, therefore, unlike the other windows in the church, it was filled with plain square-paned glass through which it was possible to see the sky and the trees beyond, the life of creation, responding to the changing seasons.

I sat down in a front pew and gazed at the cross on the altar. I thought about Bishop Robert's request. Was I ready to do this? Would it help or hinder my own journey through grief? I thought of Martin's grief when his first wife died. I had been aware of it because he had come to my parish as Archdeacon a few months afterwards, he had arrived late and all the sorrow and anguish of her loss had shown in his tired face.

I also remembered a story he had told me about Marjorie Ross who had helped out at the Old Rectory after Elizabeth's death. She was a worshipper at Chedd, the widow of a diplomat, and she had been kneeling at the eight o'clock service when the Vicar prayed for Martin and the children, and she had distinctly heard a voice say, 'Please help'. She looked around, but no-one was sitting near her, and all present were bowed In prayer. So she had gone to the Vicar later on and told him about it, wondering whether she should offer to help at the Old Rectory. The Vicar had gone to see Martin and Marjorie Ross had begun going in on some weekdays to shop and wash and iron and cook evening meals, in return for a contribution to the St.

lement's Church fabric fund. She had 'retired' from this generous labour just before
ur marriage, and I had gone to see her to thank her for all that she had done. She
vas a sensible, kind, practical woman who had spent years hosting events at various
embassies. She had believed that God was calling her to do something, and she had
done it.

Bishop Robert had come to see me, and I was plan A. This church and its people
needed a priest. No voice said, 'Please help' to me, but it was not necessary, for the
Bishop had asked me.

On my way out of the church I enquired of the elderly gentleman whether Bereston
Hall still existed. 'No,' he said, 'The estate was next to the church, but the house is
ong gone, and a lot of the land has been built on. Thank you visiting today.'

Thank you,' I said, 'It's a lovely church.'

thought it was very likely that I would see him again, quite soon.

went home and composed and sent an email to Bishop Robert to tell him that I
vould be happy to take on the role. He replied promptly saying that he was very
pleased and so I met with the churchwardens, Angela and Dennis, and we drafted a
hort statement to the effect that I would be the most regular person on their rota to
ake the Sunday Parish Eucharist, and the seasonal services, that I would not take
aptisms, weddings or funerals but that I would be available in the case of spiritual
eed.

And so it was that in October, three Sundays after my visit, I took my first service at Bereston Church, which happened to be Harvest Festival. I could not help wondering in the preceding days whether Jason would suddenly return, and plan A would not be needed after all. But nothing happened, and although I felt nervous taking a service in a church I had never functioned in, whose congregation were very worried about their own priest, and while I myself was still grieving, I was struck by two things that sustained me: the Anglican liturgy, authorised, printed and blessed by constant prayerful use, and the generous friendliness of the congregation, some of whom said, as they shook my hand and left the church, that they had been so very sorry to hear of Martin's death because he had been a wonderful Archdeacon.

VIII

When you marry someone who has been happily married and then widowed, you have one particular task before you: how you relate to the first wife. Elizabeth had been married to Martin for twenty-four years when she died, she had borne him three children and she had brought inherited wealth to the life of someone who had grown up in poverty and who spent the first twenty-six years of his ministerial life earning a curate's and then a parish priest's modest stipend. I also knew that Elizabeth's only job had been what we would now call 'personal assistant' to her father, a former Bishop of Tarnswell. In marrying Martin she had transferred all her devotion, ambition and purpose to enabling him to have a successful ministry. She was not a woman who endeared herself to people, but they did respect her.

Martin and Elizabeth had loved each other deeply and exclusively. I knew that there would always be an Elizabeth space in Martin's life, and times when he would be thinking of her, on the anniversary of their marriage, for instance, or of her death. I honoured that space, I hope, but I also believe that my relationship with Martin was different in one key respect: I was a working priest when we began to go out together, and although I gave up full-time stipendiary ministry when we married, I continued to exercise a ministry and a role in the Diocese distinct from being his wife. I also have what I believe Elizabeth may have lacked: a sense of humour. With Elizabeth Martin had always to be serious about his ministry; with me he didn't. As I stood at that church door and heard people praise him, it was as though I heard him say, 'There, well, I couldn't have been that bad then.' I don't think he would have said that to Elizabeth.

During our engagement and marriage I had worked hard to establish good relationships with all three of Martin's children and to negotiate the kinds of dangerous corners that can occur when a widowed father remarries. I had managed well, I thought, with only one memorable difficulty.

Sarah's daughter Beth was a toddler when I first started visiting the Old Rectory as the new woman in Martin's life, and Sarah was embracing motherhood with enthusiasm. So much so that, despite Beth having a lovely bedroom and playroom, her toys, clothes, bibs, soothers and various kinds of equipment tended to travel around the house, so that there was not one room that did not manifest some item related to her young life. I had no problem with this until after we were married. The Old Rectory was quite large in that it had space for the servants who would once have worked there; one such room had become a downstairs TV room which was rarely used because all the children had televisions in their bedrooms. Martin had thoughtfully offered me this room as a study and sitting room of my own and it was fun decorating it and bringing my desk, computer and other items to it – I had had to give so much of my furniture away when we married. It had two comfortable armchairs in it as well as an office chair and sometimes if Martin was working in his home office he would come in for a break and we'd sit in those chairs and have a coffee and talk together.

One day I came in from taking a mid-week service at Chedd to find a set of building blocks, a playmat and a discarded feeder cup on the floor. I said nothing then, I took them to the kitchen, but as time passed it happened more and more, so that at last one day I asked Sarah if she would mind if Beth did not come into that room. Sarah said, 'Okay, if you like; before you came, it was a nice room for us to chill out in, especially if Dad had a meeting in the living room.' Sooner than get into an argument, I said, 'I'm sorry to have taken it from you, but it's nice for me to have a space of my own, too.' Situations like that are so difficult, there's a price to pay if you stand your ground and another if you give way. I stood my ground.

It could not have been easy for them, but I hoped that they would all remember that I had loved their father very much and that after the dreadful loss of Elizabeth he had found happiness again with me. Now it remained to be seen how things would go on but social networking, emails and remembering birthdays and anniversaries – as Martin would have done – gave opportunities to keep in touch, as did a confirmation and a special birthday event to both of which I was invited. Abigail, now living fifty miles away with her husband and children, had already invited me over for a family lunch and said that if I wanted to I would be very welcome to spend Christmas with them, for this year they planned to be at home. I realised that I had not given any thought to what I would be doing at Christmas apart from taking one or more of the services at Bereston.

IX

Time passed and I began to be busy, for the regular Sunday worship required preparation; I was invited to a meeting of the parish's Liturgy Group to help plan the Christmas worship. I had many good friends who kept in touch. I was already meeting regularly for lunch with Louise Filmer, the designated secretary to the

Archdeacon of Wydebridge, who had worked for Martin up to his death; we had agreed that this arrangement should continue.

Soon after my first service at Bereston I received a request from the Vicar of All Saints', Eldon, to preach at their Patronal Eucharist on All Saints' Sunday, which that year fell on Sunday November the second. Having asked someone else to take Bereston's service, I agreed. The Vicar, Lytton, was a tall, thin man in his fifties who often wore a waxed green jacket and a beret; that and his rather lean face and prominent nose made him look, I thought, like a member of the wartime Free French. His parish embraced St. Eldon's Cliffs, where Jason Bell's car had been found.

There was a legend that a holy man called Eldon had landed at the foot of the cliffs many centuries before and built a chapel there. Lytton had decided to combine the patronal festival with a celebration of the legend of Eldon. The service began in the church, proceeded to the cliff-tops and concluded with lunch in the St. Eldon Hotel which at that time of year was very pleased to make its old-fashioned dining room available to fifty or so parishioners for a choice of cottage pie or vegetable pie and an ice-cream dessert.

After the service in church I walked with Lytton in the procession to the cliffs. I was glad that I had brought my cloak with me, as he had suggested, for it was breezy on the cliff top. Lytton's conduct of the final liturgy was most impressive; he recalled how Eldon had landed somewhere in this vicinity in late October and, in gratitude for his safe arrival, had then and there chosen the site of what became a small stone chapel. Sadly, it and the land where his barque had beached had been swept away in the erosion of the coast, and although some archaeological work had been done by divers, it was a dangerous area and the work was inconclusive. Nevertheless Eldon – if he did exist – had given his name to the village, the cliffs and the hotel. The parish brought both its own All Saints' banner in the procession, and another depicting an embroidered Eldon with a beard, wearing a full set of red Eucharistic vestments; he gazed solemnly at us as we remembered him, the material flapping in the wind.

When the liturgy was finished we stood looking out over the sea, glittering like crystal in the late autumn sun. Lytton said, 'It's easier when we do the Blessing of the Sea on Sea Sunday in July. But I feel that I should do this too, to mark the time of year when Eldon landed. Imagine the hazards of that journey.'

'Yes, indeed,' I said, 'I think it's a lovely thing to do. I've enjoyed it. Thank you so much for inviting me.'

'Thank you for your words this morning. You know why I asked you, don't you?'

'Is it because of Jason?'

'Yes.   I had asked him to put it in his diary; you are keeping his place for him, on Sundays, and I'm glad you are.   You know they found his car here?   It was over there.' He turned in the wind and pointed back to the layby opposite the hotel. There were a few cars there now, belonging to people unable to manage the procession. 'I thought of him, coming up here. I was at home, at the Vicarage.   He must have driven past my door. I knew him; not very well, but enough to wish… that he had stopped, and come in to see me, that I had been able to… talk to him, or just listen. Maybe I could have helped him.'

I said, 'I understand how you feel, and I'm sure that you are not alone.'

Lytton turned back to face the sea. 'I often come up here and look out, and think of him, pray for him. I think he's out there, somewhere. I think he's in the sea.'

looked out with him, over the great expanse of water. Soon, as winter came on, it would turn grey and brooding and sometimes rough, but today it was calm and the rippling surface shimmered. People were buried at sea; if this *was* Jason's resting-place, then on that day at least, it was beautiful.

X

St. Thomas' Bereston was a strong church with loyal congregations. The eight o'clock service which I sometimes took numbered on average fifteen, and the Parish Eucharist at which I usually presided at ten-thirty, around a hundred. Family attendance varied but most Sundays there were some young people to go out with the leaders to 'Young Church' and to come back and show us what they had been doing. The pattern of worship was constant: Prayer Book at eight, Common Worship at ten-thirty; there was a measure of ceremony but nothing fussy and when things went wrong I noticed that people felt able to laugh. I did not go there on Sunday evenings: the Parish had a good choir and two very competent lay readers who took Evensong between them. I sometimes conducted the Wednesday morning Eucharist at ten o'clock for about twenty people – some of them from the Belinger Almshouses - and enjoyed talking to the worshippers over the coffee served afterwards. There were other services that took place, such as a monthly Sunday afternoon 'messy church' with all sorts of craft and music and tea; a strong lay team led this and I was not needed. I was not the Rector (or Local Priest) and those who were taking on these roles or already shared in them were doing very well.

In the last year of his life Martin had tried so hard not to give in to his growing weakness. I went everywhere with him by that stage, driving him around, sitting outside meetings, in congregations, ready to help if, as sometimes happened, he felt faint. Once on our way back from a service we had laughed about a cope – a liturgical cloak – that he had been required to wear at an Anglo-Catholic church. The cope was so heavy and stiff that he told me that he did not worry about falling asleep or fainting because he knew it would keep him upright.

He never complained about his illness or the side-effects of the treatment that, in the end, did not work.

On those Sundays at Bereston I felt that the Eucharist held me up just as that cope had supported Martin. The words and the actions, the building and its contents, focussed not upon me, but upon what I represented: the priestly identity of the church as it remembered and made present the sacrifice of Jesus, and interceded for the world in that remembrance of his agony and sorrow. Following what Bishop Robert wanted I preached most Sundays, and most of those sermons were written in the preceding week; on the rare occasion when I found myself unable to produce a sermon I had past sermons stored on my computer from my years in ministry that I could redraft and use.

XI

At the Parish Eucharist one Sunday during the period when the choir came up to receive communion and the organist played, the organ made a strange vibrating sound. There followed a creaking noise as the organist changed stops and then played on. Someone asked me for prayers that day and we sat in the church together; when they had gone the organist opened the glass door – he had been waiting tactfully in the outer vestry – and he asked if I would help him as he sought to discover what had happened.

He switched on the electric 'blower', the organ pump. At a busy Sunday service the noise was hidden by the singing, but in the empty, silent church it made an eerie two-note throbbing sound; the organist went back through the doorway, opened a wooden panel under the organ pipes and disappeared into the inner workings of the instrument; then he came out again into the nave and asked me if I would mind holding down a key for him.

'Of course.' I went over to the console and sat down on the broad wooden bench before the two rows of keys. The organist pulled out a stop and then placed his finger on one of the black keys in the upper keyboard. The sound it produced was harsh, off-note and vibrating. 'Keep holding that,' he said, and disappeared once more through the door. Soon I could hear metallic sounds and the note changed, tightened up and improved. 'Ok,' the voice said from within, 'I think that's done it for now.'

I took my finger from the key; the motor of the blower continued to throb. There was a convex, adjustable mirror above the console, placed there to enable the organist to see what was happening behind him anywhere in the church. Looking in the mirror I saw the reflection of the north aisle and its monuments, and a bald figure in what looked like a black cassock, looking back towards me. I jerked away from the mirror with an involuntary cry, and looked round. I saw the aisle, the monuments and the small dark pointed door. It must have been the door that I had seen, with the pale keystone above it; a trick of the distorted convex mirror had made it look like a man.

The blower was switched off, and powered down. The organist came out, 'Are you all right?'

I turned back and swung myself off the bench. 'I'm fine, I just… Have you fixed it?'

'I think so, I don't want to get the tuners in, they are coming nearer to Christmas anyway. I think it will hold 'till then.'

I looked back into the north aisle. 'That door,' I said, 'Do you know where it goes?'

He too looked towards the door. 'That side of the church abuts what remains of the old Bereston Hall estate. It was the door for the family to come through – and that aisle used to house their private pew. I've seen a picture of it: it was a rather grand thing, with tall sides to hide them from ogling eyes, and velvet cushions. But the family is gone, the hall is gone, and the family pew went too.'

I went home and made myself some lunch. I had picked up the Sunday paper on the way. Our townhouse had its living room upstairs over the garage, and I enjoyed sitting in the window looking out over the street, turning the pages of the various sections of the paper. I had done my duty at Bereston and the rest of the day was mine.

XII

The following Sunday, forty minutes before the main Eucharist, that door in the north wall was the subject of a conversation. In asking the organist about it I had reminded him that it was a fire door when the church was in use; he had mentioned this to the churchwarden, Angela, but the key was found to be missing. Eventually it was discovered in the second and smaller of the two old metal safes in the vestry. It had been placed in the 'wrong' one.

'I'm glad you've found it.' I said.

'So am I, we'd have to get a new lock put in if we lost that. There used to be two keys but one of them never seemed to work.' She held up the key to the north door. It was typically large and heavy, a traditional church key. 'Jason may have got rid of that other key: he was very hot on clutter, he had a big clear out in his first year.' She stopped and then she said, 'Jason. I do miss him.'

'I'm sure you do, I'm sure you all do. I'm very sorry.'

'That funeral,' she said, with some bitterness, 'He had *five* funerals that week, two of them here in church. I had no idea that he was feeling...' She put her fist to her brow, and then she said, 'Well, I've gone over and over it; there's nothing I can do.'

It must be so hard for you, I thought, as a busy, resourceful woman, to have to admit that there is nothing you can do. I could only say again, 'I'm sorry.'

XIII

I went for a walk that day around Bereston and had lunch at the Bereston Arms. Among the old photographs on the walls there were several of Bereston Hall, an imposing, pedimented building. One showed a hunt gathering outside, ready to ride off across fields now largely given over to housing. I walked back to Bereston Church and through the churchyard and around the church itself to the outer wall of the north aisle. Although the brick wall enclosed what was left of the estate there was a section a short walk from the church's north door where big rusted hinges showed that a gate had once existed; now between the two sections of wall there was a barrier of just two thick wires. Through the trees and shrubs on the other side of the wire I could see brickwork covered in vegetation, and what looked like a glasshouse with broken panes. That part of the estate was overgrown, neglected and abandoned.

I was wearing a thick jacket for we were well into November now. Carefully I eased the wires apart, stooped down and clambered between them. A gust of wind hummed in the trees. I turned to face the church and saw among the leaves on the ground the remains of a path leading to the north door, the path from the long lost Bereston Hall.

'Excuse me, just what do you think you're doing?' It was a man's voice, very well spoken, military in tone. I turned. He was exactly what his voice made me expect, a man of perhaps seventy, dressed in tweeds and shiny leather boots, holding a walking stick with a wooden, carved handle. 'You do realise that this is private land?'

'I'm so sorry,' I said, 'I just wanted to take a look at this part of the church. I'll go back.'

He had now drawn level with me, and I could see his ruddy face, piercing blue eyes and white eyebrows working up and down under white hair beneath his tweed cap. His eyes dropped from mine and his manner changed; he had seen my clerical collar.

'Oh, well,' he said, 'That's all right then. Are you the new Vicar?'

It crossed my mind that if he had been a worshipper of St. Thomas' Church he would have known that Jason's title would be 'Rector' if it was not 'Local Priest'. 'No,' I said, 'I'm just helping out. My name is Dora Hind.'

'Well I'm Harries - with an 'e'. Sylvester Harries.'

We shook hands. 'I'm pleased to meet you, Mr. Harries. Do you own the estate now?'

'The Bereston Hall estate? Well, what's left of it, as you see. We're trying to get this bit cleared now, but having some trouble with the heritage wallahs. I bet you have trouble with them too, at your church.'

I nodded sympathetically, although I was not in any way involved in the care of the fabric of St. Thomas'. 'So, do you want to build here?'

'Want to sell it if we can; but those damned old buildings over there... they want to put a preservation order on them, one of them, anyway. Let a grand house go; now they're getting all bothered about a couple of old wrecks.'

'Are you fighting them?'

'Certainly am.' His voice changed. 'Fancy a cup of tea my dear? You should meet the wife. She would be interested to meet a lady of the cloth. Her grandmother was a suffragette, you know.'

'That's very kind,' I said, 'Thank you. I'd love to meet her.'

'Well, this way then.' He used his stick to beat away offending growth and I followed him to a new wall with a gate which he locked behind us. Beyond that gate the path was well-maintained and the leaf-strewn grass was succeeded by manicured lawn. We turned a corner and approached the back of his house: a post-war house, substantial enough but much smaller, I imagined, than the building that had once occupied the grounds. It was an attractive, decorative building of light-coloured brick with generous windows and, to one side, a short colonnade leading to a conservatory.

'Your house is very pretty.' I said. The garden was immaculate and its well-stocked and still colourful borders were neatly enclosed by the brick wall. There were steps to the terrace that surrounded the building and on either side stood two stone lions, stretched out with their great paws before them. They looked older than the house. 'I love the lions.'

'Came from the old gate. They dismantled it when they built those monstrosities over there.' He gestured with his stick towards the modern houses that Martin and I had seen under construction, just visible beyond the wall. I had always thought that they harmonised quite well with the village, but I said nothing.

We went round the side of the house and through a door into a tiled utility room. I asked if I should take my shoes off. He looked at them, they were flat lace ups, and he said they looked all right, but he took his own boots off, displaying green socks with a visible, expensive, label. He took my coat and placed it on a hook, and I followed him.

he house had a wide, panelled hallway with a round table in the centre bearing a
uge display of flowers, grasses and ferns.   Mr. Harries led me into a long sitting-
oom.   In a specially designed chair sat a woman who was clearly very disabled.   She
vas supported in the chair with a kind of frame that involved a contraption keeping
er head upright.   Her legs and feet – the ankles of which were twisted and swollen –
ay on a footrest attached to the chair.   Her left hand rested on the arm of the chair
eside a hospital-style wheeled table where lay a box of tissues and a feeder-cup with
 bottle of water beside it.

Katharine,' he said, 'The Vicar has come to call.   This is Dora... Hind, did you say?'

 stood in front of Katharine Harries and smiled at her.   'Yes, I'm Dora Hind.   I'm very
leased to meet you.'

he gazed back at me; I did not know whether she had understood, or even heard me.

She gets very tired,' said Mr. Harries, 'So she prefers to listen.   Do take a seat.'

 looked around the panelled room; it was like a small-scale version of rooms I had
isited in National Trust properties, except that everything in it was new and in
erfect condition.   The satin in the upholstered chairs and sofas seemed to shimmer.   I
at down on one of the chairs facing Mrs. Harries.   When her husband went out of
he room I said, 'Mr. Harries tells me that your grandmother was a suffragette.'

lthough her face was stiff with paralysis I saw some animation flicker.

I said, 'I'm very grateful to her for what she achieved.'

Mr. Harries came back in again. 'Tea is in hand.'

He sat down on a sofa. I said, 'How did you come to live here?'

'Well, we were abroad for a while and then… Katharine, poor darling, had her stroke and we came back. This place was everything we could have wanted.'

'Was it built soon after the Hall came down?'

'You're interested in buildings, aren't you?' For a moment he seemed to consider, then he said, 'There were some Bereston Hall papers in this house when we moved in and I gave them all to the Local History Room at Tarnswell Library. You can always take a look at them. But what I do know is that when the last of the male Belingers had died by the end of the war the old house passed to a cousin who took one look at it and shut it up for the next twenty years, by the end of which of course it was pretty run down. Then the cousin's son inherited the estate and he had the house demolished. It was the nineteen-sixties and nobody cared. He built this house, and eventually he sold half the land to the developer who built those houses. Then he died.'

A woman in a black dress with a frilly white apron and cap came in with a tray of tea, beautifully laid out with silver and fine china. 'This is Wendy. Wendy is from the Phillppines.' We exchanged a friendly greetlng. 'I'll be mother thls tlme, Wendy, thank you.' said Mr. Harries, in a firm but slightly jaunty voice, and Wendy bowed and left. He passed me a plate with a piece of fruit cake on it, and my tea, and pulled a small, delicate table round for me to use. He prepared the feeder cup for his wife and helped her to drink from it. My plate and cup felt so fragile that I was glad to put them down on the table.

When he was seated again he said, 'So, tell me about yourself. You say you're helping at the church. No sign of the missing chap then?'

'I'm afraid not.' I said. 'I'm taking some of the Sunday services.' Wanting to clarify my situation I said, 'My husband was the Archdeacon of Wydebridge, he died at Easter.'

Holding his cake in his hand Mr. Harries said, slowly and with feeling, 'I'm very sorry to hear that.'

'Thank you. It's quite nice to have something to do that isn't too demanding. Otherwise I might just sit around and... miss him.'

'But I'm sure you do miss him, and sadly you can't replace him, well, as a person, even if you marry again. But a Vicar can be replaced, surely; I mean, churches need leadership. Churches close, and then the buildings and the things in them are at risk. I don't go to church, but I believe that Bereston Church has some treasures?'

'It does; and Jason Bell appreciated them. Before he came to Bereston he was the vicar of a rather fine Georgian church – he did a huge amount to raise funds for its restoration.' It so happened that Martin had dedicated that work on the very day he came to see me and our relationship, which had seemed to be petering out, began again, and this time led to marriage.

'Is that so?' Mr. Harries seemed to ponder, then he said, 'He didn't leave a note. That way at least people would have known. The police came knocking on the door one day, wanting to search our garage and shed. Then they looked round the grounds and those old buildings. Didn't find anything. I have no key, you see, and the lock's rusted. I thought it must be pretty obvious he was in the sea. I mean, he left his car there, didn't he, on St. Eldon's Cliffs? Do you know, they found a body there a while ago: some fool fell and landed on a ledge with a sort of cave behind it, and when they winched him up he said he thought he'd seen something. They let someone down to take a look and found a chap who'd been missing for years, pretty well a skeleton.'

I said, 'I didn't hear about that. I do know that they searched for Jason.' But I thought how those cliffs stretched for some distance, with many shadowy caves and fragile ledges. How could they ever be sure that his body was not there? I said, 'If Jason isn't found, I think at some point they will have to end his tenure and the post will be properly vacant.'

'Let us hope so.' he said, 'You should apply, my dear.'

But my days as a parish priest were over.

XIV

A few days later I was at Tarnswell Library, a rather grand Victorian structure with doors like a saloon bar, curved and elaborately veneered and half-filled with smoked glass. I had started shopping for Christmas presents for Martin's family, and I had gone into the Library café on the first floor for the restorative benefits of a hot soup lunch.   Reading the paper afterwards over a cup of tea, I happened to glance up and saw that I was looking at the door of the Local History Room, and I remembered that Mr. Harries had said that he had donated some papers there that related to Bereston Hall.   I was curious to know more about the old house, and Mr. Harries had made a point of telling me they were there so before I left the library I checked the opening times of the Local History Room.

Two days later I went back.

Opening the door, I found myself in a comparatively small room lined with metal shelving laden with books and pamphlets and brightly coloured, clearly labelled box files of local history.   There was a long table in the middle of the room with chairs and at one side there was a computer and a microfiche machine.   The room was empty but there was a staff desk with an electric bell and a note beside it saying, 'Please ring for assistance'.   I rang the bell.   As I waited I looked up and saw a white closed-circuit television camera placed high up on the wall.

A man bearing an Assistant Librarian lanyard appeared from a door behind the desk.   I told him that I was interested in Bereston Hall in the Bereston area of Tarnswell.   He made a little affirmative signal with his hand and asked for my library card or identification.   I had not yet joined Tarnswell Library but I had a card issued at Wydebridge and I also showed him my driver's licence.   He unlocked a filing cabinet by the desk and took out a folder.   From this he took a form and gave it to me to complete while he went round the desk and over to the shelves.   I sat down at the table with the form; it was a request to examine materials only while in the room and a commitment to return them intact.   The assistant placed a shallow box-file beside me; he told me that when I had finished I could leave it on the staff desk; I thanked him and he left the room by the door he had entered.

Everything in the box-file was photocopied and numbered. There were two pen and ink drawings of the Tudor Bereston Hall, more like a large manor house, and several photographs of the later remodelled building; these included a photograph of the family gathered at the front of the house, and another of the staff gathered at the back. These photographs were dated before the Great War and I could see a butler, a housekeeper with her keys suspended from the waist of her dark dress, numerous male and female servants of varying status, and, at the back, a row of men dressed for outdoor work. I looked at the younger men: how many of them, and perhaps the women too, as nurses, went off to serve in the war? How many returned?   Another set of photocopied papers showed records of payments made to individual members of staff. The amounts seemed very small and they were paid only twice a year. How disciplined they had to be, I thought, to make that money last. But then for some of them the house provided everything: a uniform, shelter, meals, in return, of course, for long hours of very hard work.

Someone had helpfully prepared a short history of the Hall: I was most interested in its final years, and they were sad. A badly photocopied image showed the house in its very last days before demolition in the nineteen-sixties, shuttered and abandoned. Apart from the Almshouses, founded by an earlier Belinger, all that remained of the Bereston Hall era were two buildings on the edge of the estate: a brick garden store which dated back to the late eighteenth century, and a much later glasshouse. Another photocopied image showed these buildings. From what I had seen on that part of Mr. Harries' land they were now derelict.   Mr. Harries had said that his plans to sell were being frustrated by heritage officials.

The last of the photocopies was an article in the *Tarnswell Times*. Dated in January of the previous year it concerned the one hundredth birthday of a Miss Elsie Myers. As well as a black and white image of a very frail old lady flanked by two nursing home staff raising champagne glasses, there was another grainier black and white image of a little maidservant, Elsie at the age of fourteen, when she had started work at Bereston Hall in nineteen twenty-seven. It seemed that she had actually lived and worked there until the house was pulled down, when she was given a home in the Belinger Almshouses.

The last item in the box was a brown envelope whose neatly typed label read: 'Photocopies of papers donated by Mr. S. Harries in regard to Bereston Hall'. I took out the envelope and opened it.

The photocopied papers within related to the very last years of Bereston Hall. The house may have been closed up, but it and the estate were not completely abandoned. There were some pages of accounts: one dated nineteen fifty-eight showing monies paid to Miss Elsie Myers, housekeeper, to Mr. Ernest Philips, caretaker, and to Mr. Edwin Lewis, groundsman. In nineteen fifty-nine Mr. Jason West had succeeded Mr. Edwin Lewis, and in nineteen-sixty Mr. Alan Hartley had in turn taken over the role. I wondered what it was like for them, presumably still living in the staff quarters of that big house, with the other rooms and corridors, once bustling with life, silent and abandoned.

I put the papers back in the envelopes, returned all the items carefully to the box and took it with the form I had completed to the staff desk. The file that the assistant librarian had taken out was still lying there. I noticed that on the cover someone had written in felt tip pen: *User Forms 2014*. I put the box file and my completed form beside it, and I left.

XV

The following Sunday after worship I signed, as I always did, the church's 'register of services'. I believe that Henry VIII and then Elizabeth I ordered that a record be kept of all services conducted in parish churches. The service register books are usually blue and there are columns for the date, the kind of service taken, who took it, who preached, how much money was put in the plate, and any notes. On that day I leafed back through the book looking at the various signatures that marked the period between Jason's disappearance and the point at which I became the most regular Eucharistic officiant. Then I reached the pages signed by Jason himself: his handwriting was distinctive in bold black ink, his signature a flourish: *Jason Bell.*

I remembered then that one of the groundsmen at the Hall had been called Jason. It had not struck me at the time. Jason was a figure from Greek legend, I had read about Jason and the Argonauts at school, but I had not come across many Jasons; it always seemed an unusual name.

As some clergy do, Jason Bell had used the 'notes' column to record the subjects of his sermons. His titles were unconventional: 'Mary – truly a Virgin?'; 'The Trinity - formula or vision?'. On his last Easter Sunday, he had written 'Will we sacrifice our Risen King for a Quiet Life?' I rather wished that I had had the chance to listen to one of Jason's sermons. If he ever came back and returned to ministry I would try to do so.

But as I looked at the pages of the service register I saw that one last link with Bereston Hall had gone. The Funeral of Elsie Myers in St. Thomas' Church was one of the funerals that Jason Bell had taken, on the Thursday of that fateful Easter week. The following day he had gone out, forgetting that he had another funeral to take, at the cemetery. So began the cycle of events that had led to his disappearance, and, if the Vicar of Eldon was right, his death in the sea below St. Eldon's Cliffs.

Angela, the churchwarden, was in the vestry helping the sacristan to put things away. I had recently met up with her for coffee and we were getting on well. Now I turned to her and said, 'I see Elsie Myers died. I read about her one hundredth birthday and her link with the old Hall.'

Angela then told me that when Elsie was in the Almshouses children visited her for their local history project. Jason had taken her funeral at St. Thomas' although by then she was in a nursing home on the other side of Tarnswell. He had also given her the last rites because that parish was vacant. 'He was so conscientious.' said Angela.

Again, I heard the catch in her voice. I looked down at the register, at the flourish of Jason's signature. I thought, if only this could end, this period of uncertainty. Alive or dead, Jason needed to be found.

That was what Martin would have wanted.

XVI

My first profession was teaching, I taught mathematics at a Church of England secondary school that catered for all abilities. There were some gifted pupils there who loved nothing more than to juggle with figures; there were others who worked steadily and achieved the grade they needed in order to progress towards their chosen career; and then there were those who struggled, who hated maths, and who, unable to remember formulas, or engage with problem-solving, were bored by the whole subject. When I was told that maths was 'irrelevant' I would try to encourage them to see that they were actually doing maths in some form every day, and that my subject was not just about angles and bar charts but about developing the skills to approach life's problems in a logical way, step by step. I guess most of that fell on deaf ears.

This step by step approach came to the fore when, after my conversation with Angela I told Martin – I did still 'speak' to him at that time – that I was going to try to find out what had happened to Jason, that I was going to approach the matter logically and rather as one of my detective heroes or heroines would have done, forensically. Martin and I had different preferences in one particular area: I love detective television dramas, he disliked them, and if we did actually watch one together, when the denouement came he would say that it had been 'obvious all along that that was what had happened', whether or not he had really guessed who had committed the crime. His own preference had been for those cosy retro dramas that I consider to be equally if not more predictable. Teasing one another about our differences in this had been a fun part of our marriage. Now I told him that looking into Jason' disappearance was rather like reading a detective story and I was going to approach it in that way, putting the evidence together.

First I considered the known facts of the case. Jason Bell had become Rector or 'Local Priest' of Bereston in two thousand and twelve. Two years later he had forgotten to take a funeral on the Friday after Easter, April the twenty-fifth, having taken four funerals already that week. On the following Thursday, May the first, the *Tarnswell Times*, tipped off by the deceased's niece-in-law, had referred to this event, and a national paper took it up in a bigger way soon after. Jason had already apologised to all concerned, and the Diocese had contacted the local paper and an item indicating firm Parish and Diocesan support was published the following Thursday May the eighth, in the *Tarnswell Times.*

On Friday May the sixteenth, (the same day as Martin's funeral) Jason had driven to St. Eldon's Cliffs and left his car locked up in a layby with the keys under the front wheel. The owner of the St. Eldon Hotel saw the car draw up, but turned away from the window and saw nothing else.

then gathered the facts I knew about Jason, with the additional help of the ockfords Clerical Directory which lists the histories of serving clergy of the Church of ngland. Jason was born in 1960. He had told his congregation that he had been dopted soon after birth by a couple who were now both dead. He never married and ter five years employed by a charity he began his three-year training for the dained ministry, being ordained deacon in nineteen ninety-two and priest in neteen ninety-three. In nineteen ninety-five he had gone to be the Vicar of a arish that included a very significant but run-down Georgian church, and he had orked hard to restore it and to bring it into contemporary life. Seventeen years later e had taken up the post at Bereston at the age of fifty-two.

then considered and recorded anything that had happened that might have fluenced Jason's state of mind. I knew that his former training incumbent, friend nd mentor, Father Hilton Denyer, had died in two thousand and thirteen; it was, owever, a peaceful death at the end of a long life, well-lived. Holy Week and Easter unday would have been intensively busy for Jason and the fact that a number of inerals were booked for him to take in Easter week prevented him enjoying the rest e deserved, and needed. He had known or met at least one of the people who had ied for he had visited her on her deathbed in the week before Holy Week began. his person, Elsie Myers, was connected with Bereston Hall. Was that in any way gnificant?

then listed some questions:

Jas the missed funeral the *only* reason why Jason vanished?

Jas Jason already depressed about other things – the changes in the way the arnswell Parishes would be run and the many meetings he had to attend?

Was he more deeply affected by Father Hilton Denyer's death than he showed? Had they been more than friends? The age gap would seem to indicate that this was a professional friendship and a spiritual bond, and nothing more.

Was he involved in a relationship that no-one knew about? Was he gay? Was there something worrying him associated with that possibility?

Was there anything more to add? I remembered that Sunday when I had sat at the organ console and thought that I saw, in the mirror, a bald man dressed in a black cassock. I had assumed that I had seen the gothic door, but maybe I hadn't. Whatever I had seen, it had led me to find out more about Bereston Hall. So now I listed what I knew about the Hall and its occupants.

Bereston Hall was a Tudor manor house owned by the Belinger family, and rebuilt as an eighteenth-century Hall in what was then the village of Bereston. The male Belingers died out after World War II and a cousin, presumably with a different name, inherited the estate but stayed away and the Hall stood more or less empty for something like twenty years after the war, occupied only by Elsie Myers and one or possibly two other members of staff. The cousin then left it to his son who had the Hall demolished in the nineteen-sixties, built a smaller house and eventually sold off part of the estate to a developer. On his death without issue it was bought by Mr. Harries who now wanted to sell some of the land near the church but was having trouble because of the heritage status of the old outbuildings that once related to the Hall. Had any of this involved Jason?

The information that I recorded thus far had come to me because it was already in the common domain, if you knew where to look or whom to ask. The following day I decided to be cautiously proactive: I wrote a letter to Phillppa Blane, the wife of retired Bishop Giles Blane, now living in Somerset. Philippa and Giles had remained close friends with Martin and kept in touch with us. Philippa had nominated me for the role of stand-in Sunday priest at Bereston, and I was grateful to her for that, and for her sympathetic and sensible listening ear in the past. I decided to write and thank her, and indicate in a roundabout sort of way that I wished I knew more about Jason, because Martin would have been very worried about him. Did the Blanes know anything that might throw light upon what had happened?

Philippa sent me a prompt email by reply. She had not, as I already knew, made a point of mixing a great deal with the Diocesan clergy, and she had never known Jason himself except by sight, but she had asked Giles, and he had told her that when he learned of Jason's disappearance, he had felt that he should contact his successor to say that from his own knowledge of Jason in the past he was an excellent priest, but also perhaps a loner, a tendency that might make him more vulnerable to being hurt by the public criticism that came after the missed funeral. Philippa said that Giles remembered that when the building and restoration work had been going on in Jason's previous church he had faced some opposition and had asked for Martin's support, which Martin gave. The work went ahead and there were no further complaints but Martin had told Giles that he was aware that Jason was personally very hurt, and even depressed by some of the criticisms at the time, though when the work was complete and generally well-received, he was very happy, even elated. He was someone who experienced the highs and lows of life more acutely than others. This was nothing new.

But then Philippa had added something else: at a Diocesan clergy conference one of the readings in a Bible study had been the story in the Book of Exodus about Moses, the baby hidden by his mother in a basket in the reeds to save him from the Egyptians who were killing Hebrew baby boys. Giles was in the same discussion group as Jason and at some point Jason had said that he was rather like Moses, for he was left in a basket, not in a river but on a farmhouse doorstep. When one or two in the group had expressed curiosity he had said that all he knew was that it was a farm just outside Bereston in Tarnswell. The farmhouse people found him and looked after him, but they weren't allowed to keep him, and he was adopted.

That Jason was found in a basket on a doorstep near Bereston was very significant information, for it meant that there was a chance that his mother was or had been local to the parish where he had spent his final two years. People who were adopted now had the right to look into the details of their adoption; many made contact with one or both of their birth parents, sometimes happily, sometimes not. But Jason had been abandoned; his mother and father were unknown. They might have lived somewhere within reasonable distance of that farmhouse and have known that the family would, in the first instance, look after the child. Had the person who had left the baby stayed hidden, like Miriam, Moses' sister, to see what would happen when the basket was found?

A theory was beginning to form in my mind, drawing all these details together. But would they really fit, or was I just trying to make a coherent whole out of totally unrelated parts?

I remember reading about the discovery of the structure of DNA, the basic building blocks of life, the double helix. Several scientists had been engaged in this quest, especially a woman who was very diligent; her method was to take x-ray photographs – at considerable personal risk in those days – study them, and use methods of calculation to form her opinion. Others took a different approach. They were as scientific as she but they formed a theory about the structure of DNA and then studied the evidence – her evidence – to test their theory. They made mistakes along the way, but they got there first.

In detection, there are I imagine similar methods of working. Some detectives will build a case slowly, relentlessly, based on evidence, making no assumptions; others

ollow a hunch and see whether the evidence fits. I had not known Jason. I was
uilding up evidence to try to discover what might have happened to him, and a
heory was beginning to emerge. Such theories take shape when we allow the brain to
mull over a range of information: direct and indirect, heard and overheard, relevant
and irrelevant. I lay awake thinking that night, I got up for a while and looked at my
notes, lay awake again and finally slept.

XVII

he next day I went to Bereston Church in the afternoon when I knew it would be
locked up, using the key I had been given to go inside. I knelt at the rail before the
altar: 'If there is anything here that I should see', I prayed, 'Show it to me.' I was
praying to God, but there was in my mind a thought that Martin too might be
listening.

I walked around the quiet interior just as I had done on my first visit, letting the
building speak to me. I passed through the nave, the chancel, the south vestry aisle
beyond the beautiful glass door, and the north aisle. I studied the memorials again:
the names and the words. I looked at the tribute to James Belinger, lost at the Battle
of Loos in the Great War: *'He has gone to be with his fathers'*, and at the plain
memorial to Mary Belinger, the last it seemed to bear the family name, but not male,
not deemed worthy to inherit: *'Grant her safe lodging, a holy rest, and peace at the
last'*. I hoped that she been granted 'peace at the last'. She had died so young, had
her life been troubled and sad, that it was felt appropriate to use those words? I felt
sure that they came from one of the prayers in the funeral service.

For some time I sat in the quiet of that church, looking, listening and thinking.

XVIII

At home I used the computer to search for the words on Mary Belinger's memorial, *'grant her a holy rest and peace at the last'*. In the original, 'her' was 'us' and they had been composed by the nineteenth century Anglican priest, eventually Roman Catholic Cardinal, John Henry Newman, in a prayer that began *'O Lord support us all the day long of this troublous life'*. Was not this sentiment, I thought, very similar to that in prayer in the service of Compline or Night Prayer? There was a form of this for the Church of England and it was quite common for churches to have evening Compline in Lent and Advent, the seasons of penitence. I found my copy of the service, a green booklet, and opened it. The words were different for this modern version but the meaning was the same: *'Grant to us Lord a quiet life and a perfect end.'*

I went to sleep, and woke very early. I remembered what I had been thinking about before I slept. I remembered the words of the compline prayer about a quiet life, and now I remembered what Jason had preached about on Easter Sunday, before everything went wrong. A quiet life. *'Will we sacrifice our Risen King for a Quiet Life?'*

Had Jason been asking his congregation that question, or himself? I could imagine what he might have said: we might ask for a quiet life, but did Jesus, our King, have such a life? Did he promise that for us? No. It was one of the strange paradoxes of Christianity; Jesus once said, 'I come not to bring peace but a sword'. He knew that his message was not about quiet lives and perfect ends. Yet still that is what we pray for, because we are human, because we are afraid.

Like so many young men of his generation, James Belinger had gone to fight in the Great War, leaving a quiet life behind. What suffering had he endured before he died? Had he been afraid? The word *'lost'* in his memorial indicated that he might have been reported missing, one of the millions of men 'missing presumed died of wounds'. That was perhaps the reason why they had chosen those words beneath: *'He has gone to be with his fathers'*: they eased the agony of not knowing his fate, his final resting-place.

Then I remembered: Jason too was missing.

I spoke the words quietly in the silence: *He has gone to be with his fathers.* It seemed as though a voice whispered them back to me.

It was then that I realised that I needed but one more piece of information to give me the confidence to believe in my theory, and to put it to the test.

XIX

There was an eerie repetitiveness at the Local History Room at Tarnswell Library on the following Monday. Everything looked exactly the same as it had before: there was the bell on the desk, and when I rang it the same door opened and the same man came in. I could see that he recognised me. This time I asked for information about Tarnswell House, now the home of the Bishops of Tarnswell. Tarnswell House was still standing and the assistant located a book and some papers bound in a plastic file.

It is sometimes said that the brain never replicates an action, it approximates it: that is why, I suppose, that even the greatest tennis player can serve a double fault. Would the assistant do what *he* had done before? Would he retrieve the file called *User Forms 2014* from the filing cabinet and take out a new form for me and leave the folder on the desk? I had made an assumption that the number of people using the Local History Room would not be great: today and on the previous occasion that I had visited it the room was empty and the assistant librarian came from somewhere else. Most people would do their research on their home computer. The significant question was, would the used forms be stored with the unused ones? Those forms contained personal details: names and addresses; they should not be left unattended; it might be that they were stored in another file.

It was, however, worth acting on a hunch.

When the assistant had left the room I sat down with the form and the items he had given me. I read everything about Tarnswell House: who had built it, how it came to be given to the Diocese for the use of the Bishops, which Bishops had lived in it. I saw their pictures including a copy of a painting of Elizabeth Hind's father. He looked severe: it was strange to think that my husband had known him not only as his Bishop but as his father-in-law. We had never spoken of him.

Forty-five minutes later I took the items back to the desk; the *User Forms 2014* folder was still lying there and I placed the items that I was returning squarely upon it. Then I acted out a little pantomime for the benefit of the security camera, pretending that I had thought of something, and picking up the Tarnswell House items again, ensuring that I picked up the *User Forms 2014* file as well. I sat down away from the edge of the table with my back to the camera, re opened the plastic file and studied some detail in it. But my other hand eased the *User Forms 2014* file out and onto my lap. I opened the flap: the unused forms were on the top, but underneath, as I had hoped, were the used forms, and there were not many. It was easy to draw them out beneath the table, where I could look through them. Nor did I have to go back very far, for only seven people had visited the room to study documents since someone else came to study the information about Bereston Hall, on Friday, April the twenty-fifth. The name was in block capitals, but it was not Jason *Bell*, it was Jason *Belinger*. I looked for the address: perhaps there was, after all, a surviving male Belinger. Then I saw in block capitals, 'Diocesan Office, Tarnswell'. At the very end of the form in a familiar flourishing hand was the signature: 'Jason Belinger'.

I put everything together and carried the folders to the desk. I pretended then to realise that I had picked up the additional file, and placed it apart from the material that I had borrowed. I placed my own completed form on top of the *User Forms 2014* file on the desk.

I left the room and walked past the café and down the heavy wooden staircase of the library feeling like a criminal. But I had not taken anything, and I did not think that my inspection of the *User Forms 2014* file could have been seen by the camera. I wondered whether the camera was real and if the footage was ever examined. Presumably only if there were suspicions that something had been taken.

But none of those concerns mattered beside the fact that I now knew that Jason Bell, for it must have been Jason Bell, had studied the Bereston Hall papers on Friday April the twenty-fifth, the day that he was supposed to take the funeral that he had forgotten about, and the day after he had taken the funeral of Elsie Myers. He had signed himself, 'Jason Belinger'. It was, indeed, the missing piece of my theory and it was a bigger and more significant piece than I had imagined.

Should I go to the police with my theory? In my mind, I saw myself going to the desk at Tarnswell Police Station, asking to see someone involved in the case of Jason Bell, the missing priest from Bereston, whose car had been found in a layby on St. Eldon's Cliffs. I saw a kindly helpful detective listening to my story, asking his colleagues for information about the search for Jason. I saw him agreeing to arrange another search, this time with the kind of ramming device you see on those news stories of police breaking open the door of a criminal's home in an unwelcome early call.

But then I remembered an incident at my parish at Wydebridge Green when someone had left a sports bag containing a silver tea-set and a box of jewellery in a sheltered corner behind St. Mark's Church. I had rung the police at Wydebridge and a rather bored-sounding officer had said, 'Do you mind bringing it in?' Of course I took it in to them, but it felt as though I had interrupted more important work, and probably I had. What would the Tarnswell police make of a woman priest with a theory about a missing colleague? Would I receive unwelcome attention myself? In any case, I might be completely wrong.

Then it occurred to me that there was another way.

XX

The following day I rang Mr. Harries' home. Wendy took the call, and said, 'One moment, please, I will see if Mr. Harries is at home.' When Sylvester Harries came to the phone, I asked him if I could pay him a visit. 'May I know in advance what it is about?' said the familiar military voice.

I decided to be direct. 'It's about Jason Bell. I have a theory. I would like to share it with you.'

There was a silence, then he said, 'How intriguing. Do come round.'

went that afternoon.

Catharine Harries was asleep in her chair. Sylvester Harries listened, his head on one side, his blue eyes fixed on me, as I told him my story. Then he sat back in his chair and considered. 'So,' he said, at last, 'Should we call the police?' I was about to reply when he held up his hand. 'No.' he said, 'We won't. This is *my* land, and those outbuildings belong to me. I've never been able to get into that old garden store; the lock is rusted up, and there's no key, and frankly I don't particularly want to, but I suppose I should. I think it's time I got a locksmith out: after all, if those heritage people want to preserve it they'll need to be able to get into it first, and see it.'

'Yes,' I said, 'That's right. Thank you.'

I did use a man when we took on the house, we changed all the locks of course. I'll see if he can help, or if he knows someone who can. It's a bit specialised, isn't it, as locks go?'

I agreed, but I felt strange and almost afraid; now that my theory had been shared it seemed foolish and wild. But Mr. Harries had thought of that; as he said, the heritage people would one day need to get into that building, so it should be opened.

Instead of going home, I drove to the little churchyard opposite Tarnswell House at Tarnswell Highfields, and I visited Martin and Elizabeth's grave. The stone had been removed when Martin was buried, and taken away so that his name and dates could be placed beneath Elizabeth's.

In the last year of his life Martin had often felt cold, although the Old Rectory was well heated. He took to wrapping himself up in the soft grey chenille throw we put on our bed when it was not in use; one day I had come home to find him wrapped up in that way, and sitting in my study on one of the armchairs with his feet on the other, and a fan heater on at its highest setting. I brought in some tea and Martin said that he had suddenly wanted to feel close to me; then he asked me about his burial. Calmly, I said that I would do whatever he wished, because I remembered that he had once said something about not wanting Elizabeth to lie alone. He wanted to be buried with her with the same simple memorial and I reassured him that I wanted that too, and that that would happen. The grave was double depth – he had not thought of remarriage when he buried her.   Whatever my own feelings I wanted him to feel settled about the details that would follow his own death.   Eventually we went into the sitting-room and he lay on the big sofa there and I sat beside him with his head resting on a cushion in my lap. That evening I contacted the Diocese and our local Vicar and told them that I would be unable to take any more services.

Now the stone was back, and I looked at the neat grass-covered grave and the words on the headstone: *'Elizabeth Anne Hind, 1948-1997',* and then *'Martin Hind, 1949-2014'.* Martin had no middle name. I thought of the words I had once heard or read somewhere: *'We give them back O Lord. We give them back to you.'*

XXI

Mr. Harries rang me that evening. 'Been trying to reach you Vicar,' he said, 'I don't care to leave messages. Chap's coming on Thursday, around eleven. Can you be there?'

'Yes, and thank you, I would very much like to be there.'

The following day I had a surprise visit from Sarah, Martin's eldest daughter.

Sarah was now thirty-nine. I had not known her mother well, but people often commented on the likeness between Sarah and Elizabeth. We went into the sitting room where she sat on the sofa. I complimented her new hairstyle: her long thick near-black hair had been cut, thinned and shaped in a feathery way that softened a face that sometimes looked severe. She was wearing smart jeans, boots and a knitted smock that had a South American look about it. I made coffee and brought it in.

'I hope I've not come at a bad time.' said Sarah.

'Not at all. It's really nice to see you. How is Beth?'

'She's fine. She amazes me, she works so hard. She's more like Abigail than me.' Beth was in her first year of A-level studies. Sarah and Beth had moved to a rented flat in Tarnswell when she was still at primary school and Sarah, a history graduate, had got a job in the libraries and heritage department of Tarnswell City Council. After a year this job and the money her mother had left to each of her children enabled her to buy a beautifully restored old terraced house with a small garden in the city.

Martin had missed Sarah and Beth being around at the Old Rectory, but he had been glad that Sarah was moving on. 'She's very bright, you know,' he had said to me; 'I love Beth and I wouldn't want her not to be with us, but Sarah's life took a funny turn after Elizabeth died, and I'm glad to see it getting back on track.' Sarah had taken various jobs over the years of Beth's early childhood: she had worked in the little local shop at Chedd, and she had marked public examination papers. Now her life was indeed going forward: she was progressing in her career and she had made many friends in Tarnswell.

It occurred to me now that she probably knew all about the outbuildings at Bereston and the Local History Room at Tarnswell Library. I mentioned the fact that, helping at Bereston Church, I had become more aware of the former estate. 'Oh yes,' she said 'There was something about that, to do with those old buildings. But it's all gone quiet now. Anyway, I had a letter with me to deliver if you were out, but I'm glad you're in.'

'Me too,' I said, 'It's good to see you.'

'I have some news.' She hesitated and for a moment I wondered if this was news that would in some way trouble me. 'I'm going to get married.'

I was both surprised and pleased. Neither before nor since her father's death had there been any mention of a new man in her life. I said, 'Congratulations, Sarah! I'm very happy for you.' Martin had once said that she was always secretive about relationships: it was only when Beth started school that he was told who her father was, a pleasant young man from Wydebridge, with whom Sarah had once been close, now married with children but who had turned out to be a good father to his unplanned eldest daughter.

Anticipating my question, Sarah said, 'Thank you. He's a colleague – he works in the housing department, in fact he runs it. His name's Stewart, spelt with a 'w'; I really want you to meet him.'

'I'd love to meet him.' I said, 'And your father would have been very happy for you.'

Sarah pulled back slightly on the sofa and looked down at her mug of coffee.   Then she placed the mug carefully on the coaster on the table beside her.   Had I spoken out of turn?   I had once had a conversation with a woman whose step-mother had just died, a few years after her father.   At one point she had said, quite forcefully, 'You know, I feel I've got my father back at last.'   Did Sarah feel that she now had Martin back?   Was I being presumptuous speaking for him?

I said nothing, and then Sarah said, 'I'm not too sure about that. You see, Stewart's divorced.'

'Would that have worried Martin so much?' I said.   'The Church allows divorced people to remarry if...'

She looked up brightly at me. 'Oh no, it's not that. We won't be marrying in church. But I did wonder... anyway, the thing is, he left his wife for me. I mean he might have left her anyway, but he was still living with her when we got together.'

I said, 'I see what you mean, I'm sorry I misunderstood.'   I wondered for a moment why she had chosen to tell me this, since she did not have to.   Wanting to move the conversation on I said, 'How long have you known Stewart?'

'Long enough.' she said. 'It's all been quite hard for him.   He didn't move in with us, I think you should know that.   He left his wife and rented a place, not much more than a bedsit.   But now the divorce is through, and we're planning to marry, he has moved in.'

'Does Beth like him?'

'It's a bit tricky; you see she's friends with his eldest daughter and her father leaving rather affected her GCSE's. She didn't do very well. She's sided with her mother and she doesn't speak to her father and now he's living with *us*… it's difficult for them. But actually, in spite of that, Beth likes him. He really is a very nice guy.'

I felt for Beth in that situation, trying to work out her loyalties; 'I'm sure he is. Does he have other children?'

'Three. The eldest boy's away at university; he won't see his Dad either, at the moment. There's a twelve year old girl, and a four year old boy. They're always glad to see him.'

'And his former wife?' I knew at once that I should not have asked that question; it came out of my professional instinct: if a divorced person sought re-marriage it was a question that had to be asked. But not now.

Yet Sarah answered with characteristic honesty: 'Pretty angry and upset. So you see, Dad might not have liked it very much. He would probably have given me a sermon.'

That comment annoyed me, but I was careful not to show it. I wanted to say that the fact that Martin was a priest did not mean that when he gave his children his opinion it had to be seen as a sermon. But I also knew that it was something that they had always joked about among themselves, and that I should not interfere.

I also knew that Sarah was thinking of the Church's – Jesus' – teaching on marriage, that it was lifelong; yet that teaching had been interpreted in practice to accept the reality of marital breakdown and divorce, and the hope of a second chance. It did not, however, condone the painful truth of one person's, in this case, Sarah's, happiness meaning someone else's hurt and loss.

As if she knew what I was thinking, Sarah suddenly looked at me intently, and said, 'Tell me this, Dora. You married my father after my mother died. I know that that was completely different, but, weren't you ever *glad* that she had died?'

I said, 'That's difficult Sarah.' I sat and thought about it, and then I realised that I was doing what she thought clergy always did, concealing painful truths behind crafted sermons. I said, 'If I was glad about anything, it was that, when your mother was dead, and your father was looking for companionship again, he asked me out. I am glad about that. ' Then I said, 'It isn't what we feel for people, it's what we do about it that matters.'

I knew the truth of it; I knew that I had felt something for Martin even when Elizabeth was alive; but when Elizabeth died it was his initiative, not mine, that had brought us together. I did not feel able to speak of this to Sarah, and in so holding back I was less honest with her than she had been with me. There was, after all, something right about Sarah's criticism of the clergy.

Sarah sat silently for a moment; then she said, 'Well, I did think that it might be nice... to have a blessing. Not straight away, later on. Would you... could you do that for us?'

'Of course.' I said, 'I would love to do it.'

I felt wretched when she had gone. Here she was embarking on a marriage with a man who had left his wife and four children for her, and she had managed to make me feel guilty for the love I had borne her father and the happiness we had enjoyed. But was that really what she had intended? Bereavement is strange territory. After Sarah had gone I wept not just tears of sorrow, but of anger, the kind of helpless anger we always feel for those who have the power to make us betray ourselves, or let ourselves down.

XXII

On Thursday I went to the Harries' house just before eleven. I sat with Mr. Harries in the living room, his wife was, again, asleep. 'Poor old girl,' he said, 'You know, it's so hard when you can't help someone.'

I said something to the effect that I thought that he did everything he could, but I did not really know what to say.

He did not look at me when he said, 'But I mean, *help* someone.'

I was relieved when there was a distant knock on the front door and then the bell rang. Wendy showed in a well-built, cheerful man wearing jeans and a zipped jacket with a logo and carrying a toolbox.

Ir. Harries rose to his feet. 'Good of you to come.' he said. They shook hands. 'The car's called in too. Shall we go?' He turned and indicated that I should follow.

e led the way into the hall and out through the tiled utility room where he handed ie my coat, put on his own tweed jacket, changed his slippers for the shiny boots, nd collected his stick. Soon we had passed through the new gate and were walking silence on the leaves, grass and twigs of the land between his garden and the urch.

At last among the trees we saw the brick store and the broken-down glasshouse. he locksmith and I waited as Mr. Harries went forward, thrashing the undergrowth side. The glasshouse looked beyond redemption: part of it had completely ollapsed, almost every window was broken. The old garden store looked more ibstantial, red brick and tiled roof just visible beneath the vegetation, heavy wooden oor, doorknob and big old rusted lock. It looked long-disused and forgotten. I began o think that I had made a mistake.

've done one of these before.' said the locksmith. He tested the door to see if was uly locked, turning the knob and pushing hard against it. My. Harries stood, arms lded, stick hooked over his arm, watching. The locksmith put his toolbox down on e damp ground, opened it and produced a can of oil. He put some of the oil into the ck, and then he worked away with items from his toolbox. We stood waiting. I oked over at the north wall of the church, at the wire between it and the land, and t the disappearing path.

here was a grating, cranking sound. The locksmith said, 'I think that's done it.'

'Well done that man!' said Mr. Harries. The locksmith was turning the knob again, and pushing the wooden door open. The hinges were stiff and rusted and the door had slipped; it scraped on a stone floor and stopped. He stood back, and moved away.

'Care to take a look Vicar?' said Mr. Harries. To my surprise he took a small torch from his pocket and handed it to me.

I moved forward. I lay my hand flat against the roughened wood and managed to push the door a little further open, feeling its resistance. When there was space enough for me to enter, I switched on the torch and I went in.

The interior of the building seemed empty: I saw rough-hewn wooden partitions and shelves: the tools and implements once stored there had long been disposed of. Then I saw a gleam of whiteness to the right, and moved the light towards it: it was a very large wooden sign painted in white and faded colours with the words 'Parish Summer Fete', and some other details; it was leaning against the wall, layered in dust and cobwebs. I turned and shone the torch further to my right, up and then down.

Someone had made up a sort of bed on the stone floor. Beside it I saw a lantern, a small medicine bottle, a book, a bottle of fruit juice and a large old-fashioned key. The bed was composed of a sleeping-bag and a pillow, and someone was in the bed, someone who had been sleeping there for a long time.

I stood quite still. I said a short prayer and a blessing, and made the sign of the cross. Then I went out.

Mr. Harries and the locksmith were talking amiably. Mr. Harries turned to me: 'Anything interesting in there, Vicar?'

I adopted the face and manner of one who has suffered a significant shock. I said, 'Mr. Harries, we need to call the police. There's someone in there, and he's dead.'

XXIII

The police came and soon the area around the two outbuildings was cordoned off and busy with men and women in protective clothing.

I gave a statement there and then, in the kitchen where Wendy provided cups of tea. I told them that I had called on Mr. Harries that morning before the locksmith had arrived. Mr. Harries knew that I was interested in old buildings and invited me to go with them. He had suggested that I take a look inside and I had found the body. It was a shock, yes, but I had seen dead people before and most of the body was covered up. I would be all right.

I was not an important witness. I drank my tea down and was told that I could go. I knew that if Mr. Harries chose to tell them what I had told him, then they would call me back; but they never did. On the day Jason Bell probably died in Bereston I was miles away in Chedd, preparing to attend my husband's funeral. Nor was any link ever made between my use of the Local History Room and the events of that day.

The coroner ruled an open verdict, although there was no evidence that anyone else had been involved. Jason had left no note, but there was the empty bottle that had contained powerful sleeping capsules, and the half-drunk bottle of fruit juice. The label indicated that the capsules had been prescribed for Jason a few years earlier. It was not known exactly how many had been in the bottle, but it was enough to put him to sleep forever. The other items were the battery-operated lantern, the heavy old key to the garden store, which had once been kept in the church safe, and the book. The book had been given to him, so the inscription said, by Father Hilton Denyer. It was a book of readings for the guidance and encouragement of the young priest.

I was given all these details by Bishop Robert.

It was fortunate that the vegetation covering the roof had prevented the theft of the tiles, so keeping the body dry and less distressing to behold. I had not looked long at the face on the pillow, a face like a mummified pharaoh, but I had seen enough to know that it was Jason from that photograph pinned on the noticeboard in the church porch.

I told the Bishop that I had offered a short prayer of commendation and a blessing, and made the sign of the cross. He seemed glad to know that.

He came to see me soon after the body was found. On the Sunday following the discovery he had set aside what he was doing to officiate at the Parish Eucharist at Bereston and formally announce Jason's death. Rumours had been flying but I had refused to say anything except that I had been present when the discovery was made.

The Bishop informed me about the arrangements for Jason's funeral and said that after an appropriate time the vacancy would be declared and the process of reappointment begin. If I felt able to carry on until the new appointment took effect he would be very happy, and he knew that the folk at Bereston would be too; he also wondered if I might like to establish an ongoing presence at that church, as an associate priest. This of course would depend upon the wishes of the next incumbent. I said that I would give that some thought. Part of me wondered whether he wanted me to apply for the post.

I had not told Mr. Harries the whole of my theory: just enough to make him feel that it might be a good idea to get into the garden store. He, sensibly I thought, had made arrangements that had nothing to do with me, but ensured that I was there. In the event he told the police that he had already looked into selling that part of his land, that there were heritage issues, and that because he had no key he had decided that he would get a professional locksmith to open the door so that he could see what was inside. He knew that I liked old buildings and had therefore suggested that I go in first.

He reminded them that the police had searched his land when Jason disappeared: they had looked into the broken-down glasshouse, but they had been put off the store by the rusted lock and the absence of a key, for, as far as Mr. Harries knew, the key had been lost for years. Someone at the station would probably be told off about that. Once Jason had identified the other key in the church safe, and made it work, he could go in and out of the garden store without Mr. Harries – or anyone - knowing about it.

I thought long and hard about whether I should share my theory with the police, or the Bishop. In the event I kept it to myself, and here it is:

Jason Bell was born in nineteen sixty. His mother was Mary Belinger and his father was Jason West. Mary was probably the last surviving Belinger but it may have been that her mental health was not strong. I did not know how she had died. In nineteen fifty-nine the greater part of Bereston Hall was closed up, but there were three people still looking after the estate: a housekeeper, a caretaker and a groundsman. I imagined that the successive groundsmen were local men, taking the job for a year or so and moving on; the other two still lived in the service wing of the Hall.

At some point Mary Belinger visited the Hall, perhaps to see Elsie Myers, and she became pregnant by Jason West. By the time she gave birth, someone else was the groundsman, and Mary died after her child's birth. Before or after her death her baby was left on a farmhouse doorstep by Elsie. The family at the farmhouse was known to be kind-hearted: whoever left the baby assumed that they would take him in, and perhaps believed that they would be able to keep him. The authorities prevented that and Jason was adopted. There had been some letter or label in the basket informing them that his name was Jason Bell: Jason for his father and Bell for Belinger. It was most unlikely that anyone would discover his parentage, and if they did, Mary was dead, and Jason West had been replaced.

Jason Bell was brought up by adoptive parents who let him keep his given name, and told him when the time was right that he had been left on a farmhouse doorstep near Bereston, and taken into the care of the local authority before they had adopted him. He was never therefore able to locate his true parents, although he may have looked for the farmhouse, if it still existed. There were several older buildings in the new housing estates built on farmland between Bereston and the coast.

Jason had formed a close bond with his training incumbent, Father Hilton Denyer. He remained unmarried. He brought many gifts to his ministry including a love of churches and of heritage, and an enquiring, open mind; he was a loner by nature, and subject to depression and insomnia, and therefore vulnerable to personal criticism.

In the week before Holy Week in his last year, Jason had been called to a nursing home to attend a dying woman, Elsie Myers, who had once lived in his parish. It is uite possible that she told Jason the story of the baby left in a basket on the armhouse doorstep. She had done this perhaps for the baby's safety and well-being, nd she had hoped that he would be taken in by the kindly family at the farmhouse. he had not realised that that would not happen, and perhaps she always believed hat what she had done was wrong. Jason only visited her at the end of her life, hen she was over one hundred years old. He was not her home's regular priest. She ay have had no idea who he was.

ut now Jason knew who he was, and that a strange twist of fate had placed him in he church that had once been the neighbour of the great house he might possibly ave inherited, that might at least have been, in happier circumstances, his home. lsie died soon after; had Jason then studied the memorials in the church, had he orked out that Mary was his mother, dying in the year that he was born? Had he uessed or known from Elsie that Mary was unmarried and troubled? Had he worked ut who his father was from the list of employees in the final years of Bereston Hall?

he liturgically heavy Passiontide and Easter had been followed not by a much-eeded rest but a busy week of funerals. On Thursday April the twenty-fourth Jason ad taken Elsie Myers' funeral in St. Thomas' Church, and her burial in the churchyard, n accordance with the wishes of her will. The funeral must have affected him. riday was normally his day off; he was tired and troubled and he forgot about the last uneral. Perhaps he had resolved to try to find out who his father was, for he might et be living. He began his research at the Local History Room at Tarnswell Library, nd he discovered a name, the name that I had seen: Jason West, groundsman at ereston Hall in nineteen fifty-nine, but not in nineteen-sixty. Perhaps he had realised hen that Jason West had probably abandoned Mary, or even just moved on without nowing that she was expecting his child.

Arriving back at the Vicarage Jason had listened to his messages and in particular the panicky one from the undertaker: we are here at the cemetery, where are you? He checked his mobile phone and found the same. He had missed a funeral; everyone had been there waiting for him and he had failed to appear. It was a human error, but I think Jason felt his failure deeply, especially because of what he had actually been doing that day.

He contacted the family and the undertakers and apologised. The following week the item appeared in the *Tarnswell Times*. Then the national tabloid headline followed. The Parish and the Diocese did what they could, but the damage was done. Jason had just discovered the truth of his birth: he was the last direct child of a family whose big old house was left disused and eventually demolished; he could perhaps have been the heir to that estate, but he had been left in a basket on a doorstep with a different surname. Adopted under the name of Jason Bell, he had created a life for himself, a life of vocation and service, modelled on the example of the one person to whom he had been spiritually close, Father Hilton Denyer. But Hilton Denyer was now dead, and unable to guide him when his failure was held up for everyone to see in the words: '*Vicar's No-Show at Funeral*'.

'Will we sacrifice our Risen King for a Quiet Life?' That had been the theme of Jason Bell's last Easter sermon. Was he already considering the possibility of making a claim for some share of whatever remained of the Belinger estate? There had been funds enough to put a memorial in Bereston Church for Mary Belinger. Success in this quest might mean that he would no longer have to serve as a parish priest in a time of meetings and changes that went against his traditional understanding of his role, that he would never have to be described as the 'Local Priest' Had he also been thinking of the 'quiet life' that his mother Mary Belinger had been denied, a quiet life that her memorial had wished for her in death?

But surely making his claim would have meant entering a legal minefield. The estate had been sold; who had the proceeds of the sale? Did Jason's failure, as he saw it, as a priest, seem like a punishment for contemplating such a claim – as though he had been contemplating the sacrifice of his King for a quiet life, and in so doing had sacrificed his vocation? Jason had wanted to be a priest since the age of twenty-four and it had taken him five years of work, three years of study and a year of diaconal ministry to reach that goal. Did the missed funeral, in his troubled, weary, confused state of mind, seem to wipe out everything that he had achieved?

At some point Jason must have decided to end his life. He had found out – perhaps from some elderly parishioner - that the other big key in the safe fitted the old outbuilding in the grounds of the former Bereston estate. I had seen the old Summer Fete sign in there. Years before when the house stood abandoned and the garden store had been cleared of all but a few basic implements the church must have been allowed to use it, and still had a key. The other one – if there was another one – probably got lost when Bereston Hall came down. The church's key was in one of the vestry safes. That old store was the last real link to the actual Bereston Hall, and no-one went there. Mr. Harries may have told Jason what he had told me – that he couldn't get in and he couldn't sell the land. Jason had seen another Belinger memorial in the church, one commemorating a son lost in war, who had *'gone to be with his fathers'*. He resolved to do the same.

Jason must have spent some time quietly making his preparations. He must have gone to try the lock, and then to lay out the bedding on the stone floor. Sometime in the small hours of Friday May the sixteenth he drove to St. Eldon's Cliffs and left his car there, placing the keys beneath it. Then, probably dressed in such a way as to conceal his identity, he walked the five or six miles back to Bereston, put on his black cassock, took the key, the lantern, the juice, the book and the capsules, and let himself into the old garden store. He lay down in the sleeping bag, folding the flap over around him, with his head on the pillow. He had locked the door behind him and taken out the key; perhaps he lay there reading from the book that reminded him of a great friendship and source of inspiration, reminded him of what he truly was, a priest of the Church, before at last opening the bottle of juice and swallowing the capsules. Then he lay down to sleep, and to pass, quickly, I hope, from sleep to death.

I remembered the occasion when the organist had asked me to hold down a key and I had looked into the convex mirror and thought I saw a man in a black cassock standing by the door.   Logically I had just seen the door and confused it for a man. But had I seen a man?   Sooner or later something would have happened to that old building: someone would have got in. The thought of anyone finding Jason in that way was not a good thought. I had known what I might find, I was prepared, and I was – and am - a priest.

XXIV

Jason Bell was buried in Bereston Churchyard, not very far from the last graves of the Belinger family, including that of the woman I believe was his mother.

There was a very significant response to the discovery of his body, not only in the media and among the members of his past and present churches, but among the clergy of the Diocese of Tarnswell, who, led by the chairman of the house of clergy of the Diocesan Synod, requested permission to show their support for their dead colleague. It was decided that the hearse would take the coffin to a spot about two miles up the road towards Eldon, and from there any clergy who wished could walk behind it.   The Bishop, the churchwardens and two distant members of Jason's adoptive family led the way, and I walked behind them with the other clergy who assisted at St. Thomas'. A helicopter flew over the procession and was evidently filming it, I saw the film later on the local news and a photograph in a church newspaper and in a national paper too. For some distance behind the hearse the road was thick with the black cassocks, white surplices and white stoles of more than two hundred clergy. The traffic had to be diverted while the procession took place. When we reached the church many of the clergy and others simply stood in the churchyard in silence as the funeral and then the burial took place, and then they quietly dispersed.

For many, many years people will remember how Jason Bell came back to Bereston.

XXV

Sarah married Stewart in a quiet civil ceremony with, on her side, only her daughter Beth, her brother Jamie, her sister Abigail and her aunt Rebecca in attendance. In her letter thanking me for the card and gift I sent, she reiterated her hope that I would one day bless their wedding. I said that I would be happy to do so. I hope that I will one day hear what she and Stewart have decided about this and I wish them well.

Bereston now has a new Rector. Mrs. Harries died; her funeral did not take place in Bereston and I was not involved; her husband sold up and moved back abroad. Before he left I saw him once in Tarnswell wearing white trousers, a striped blazer and a straw boater which he raised to me. The new owners of the house eventually got permission to demolish the glass house, and to build another house ingeniously incorporating the old garden store. They moved into the new house and sold the other. So it was that the Bereston Hall estate finally disappeared. I keep in touch with Angela and she tells me that their new neighbours attend worship and support the church.

A few days before the new Local Priest or Rector was installed I took my last Sunday Parish Eucharist as regular stand-in priest at St. Thomas' Bereston; before we processed out the churchwardens came forward, made a speech of thanks and presented me with a bouquet of flowers. I thanked them and said that I had very much enjoyed being with them and wished them every blessing with their new parish priest. I greeted people for the last time at the door; as usual there was coffee available in the north aisle of the church for those who had attended the service and anyone who happened to be visiting the church.

As people began to leave I made my way to the vestry where the treasurer was counting the collection and the sacristan was putting things away. I took off my robes and came out with my bags and the bouquet of flowers to find a couple I did not recognise studying the church guide leaflet. I greeted them and when they replied I noted that they were either American or Canadian.

I closed the glass door behind me and they came over to look closely at it. 'What an unusual, beautiful thing,' the woman said, 'And how very sad, to die at fourteen.'

'I guess that's the girl herself.' said the man.

I had not noticed that there was a figure among the flowers, the trees, the birds, the animals, and the swirling writing commemorating Alina Harris. The man was right: almost hidden among long rush-like grass there was a figure of a young girl sitting on a stone lion with her arms around its neck.

I had been so interested in the Belinger memorials that, while I loved this screen, I had not examined it so closely. I saw that the stone lion was not portrayed as I knew it to be now, on one or the other side of neat well-kept stone steps; here the lion was almost concealed by long grass; this, surely, was how those lions would have looked hen Belinger Hall was still standing and the big gates were locked and the grass was owing high around them. A young girl called Alina Harris had come to Bereston efore the new estate was built and the lions removed to their present place close by e new house now occupied by Mr. Harries: not 'Harris' but 'Harries' with an 'e'. 'as that a coincidence? Alina had died young; I had not realised that her memorial d anything to do with Bereston Hall. I had assumed that she was perhaps a aughter of one of the fine houses on the green.

t that moment I heard Mr. Harries saying, as he had at our first meeting in his 'ounds by the old path to the church, 'I'm Sylvester Harries – Harries with an "e".' I w him in his tweeds with his polished boots, his expensive green socks and his arved stick, then his striped jacket and his boater. I heard his voice, his refined, ilitary accent; I saw him in that house with its perfect, new, shining, opulent rniture; I saw him giving Wendy her orders, Wendy in her old-fashioned maid's niform, I saw him as someone who was dedicated to being something that he was ot born to be. Martin's role had taken us into some aristocratic homes: they were, ɔmehow, different.

n the north side of the church there were memorials to the Belingers who had lived Bereston Hall. Mr. Harries had told me that when the last male Belinger died a istant cousin had inherited, and left the Hall to his son who knocked it down, divided e land and built the new house, which Mr. and Mrs. Harries eventually moved into. had assumed that Sylvester Harries had bought the house; I realised then that he had ever said to me, 'I bought it'; he had said, 'We took it on' and 'It was everything we anted.' If Alina Harris had lived at the new house that replaced Bereston Hall and ᴎen died young, was there another Harris, living abroad, who had inherited the ouse instead of her, and did he become Sylvester *Harries* - turning himself into a gure of the gentry while his stricken wife watched?

And if, one day, a distraught priest turned up on his doorstep and said that he had grounds to believe that he was descended from the Belingers and therefore had a share in whatever remained of their estate, that priest might not have realised that he was in fact talking to the very person who had inherited everything, whose wife was desperately ill, and who could not imagine ever letting it go. What was it that Sylvester had said to me? Husbands could not be replaced, but Vicars could be; there were fine things in Bereston Church that needed looking after. Yes, the screen was one of them, a screen dedicated to the memory of a child who was, in some way, related to him, and whose death had been so fortuitous.

Had Sylvester Harries found it possible and necessary to put Jason to sleep for ever, by telling Wendy he would make the tea, by 'being mother'? After all, had he not spoken of wanting to 'help' his wife, by which I think he meant, hasten her death, end her suffering? Had he used the capsules he kept ready for her, and placed Jason's body in the old garden store using a key which, after all, he had had in his possession all the time? Had he then taken Jason's own housekey and let himself by night with gloved hands into that Rectory at the end of the churchyard, and located, no doubt with great satisfaction, Jason's own sleeping capsules, prescribed some time before, perhaps with just one or two remaining, kept for a bad night; had he also taken the bottle of fruit juice from the fridge, the lantern Jason kept ready for a power cut and the book he always kept beside his bed? Perhaps even the sleeping bag and pillow were Jason's own. Had I been in danger when I went to see Sylvester Harries with my theory, or did he realise that it gave him the opportunity to enable Jason's body to be found and, according to his preparations, interpreted as a suicide, long enough after his death for any clever pathologist not to be able to discover any distinction there might perhaps be between the chemicals from the capsules in Jason's body and those labelled on the bottle? Was it Sylvester Harries who, after all, had driven Jason's car to St. Eldon's Cliffs and left it there? Ha he earlier parked his own car unobtrusively somewhere in Eldon village and taken a bus back, so that he could on that morning drive back to Bereston?

But why then had Sylvester Harries asked me into his house when we first met, after initially ordering me off his land? Had he been surprised and shocked to see a priest there, not far from the place where the body of Jason Bell was lying, locked away? Was there some burden of shame and guilt and fear that made him want to make some connection with the Church? Would he, one day, have confessed what he had done, just as Elsie Myers had confessed to placing the baby in the basket outside the farmhouse door, when she was on her deathbed? When he had summoned me to the house to meet the locksmith he had rung me, but not left a message. 'I don't care to leave messages.' he had said. No, especially if that message might incriminate him of engineering my discovery of the body he already knew was there.

I left the couple, I said my farewells to those still in the church, and hurried home. I left the flowers and my bags in the kitchen and sat in a chair in the sitting room in turmoil. The theories and the known facts swirled around in my head like the writing on Alina Harris' memorial. Jason had left his car at St. Eldon's Cliffs and then committed suicide in the garden store because he was depressed and did not want people to search for him; he wanted them to think that he had jumped from the cliffs. Jason had committed suicide because he had been temporarily diverted from his true path of life by his discoveries about his parentage and because of the public criticism over the missed funeral. Jason had been murdered by Sylvester Harries because he was a threat to Sylvester's new-found wealth.

I thought of my own situation. I had been so satisfied with myself: being invited by the Bishop to help out at that church, being so well-received, and then undertaking this investigation. I had been foolish and I had probably been used. My husband was dead and I was alone: his children would gradually forget me, I had no real connection with them, their father and their mother were reunited in death. I was nobody and nowhere. Nor, knowing what I knew, could I ever return to St. Thomas'. I should have handed in my key anyway after the service, had those visitors not distracted me, those visitors who had shown me the one clue that I had missed, that I wished that I had never seen.

Thinking of that church key I suddenly saw that that there one unresolved matter: the key or keys to the garden store. The store was locked from the inside and the key was lying beside Jason with, presumably, his fingerprints upon it. But there had to be another key if Mr. Harries was involved. That would of course explain why one key was lying beside the body; it would not be possible to lock the door from the outside if it was still in the lock inside. But what had happened to the key that had been kept in the church safe? Had Jason really removed it in his early declutter? Had Mr. Harries found it, perhaps on display in the Rectory, when he went in once Jason was dead? Had Jason actually taken the key to Sylvester Harries? Or had Sylvester already got two keys, and the key kept in the church had simply been discarded.

Or was my first theory in fact quite right? Jason had simply killed himself.

The keys seemed to swim around in my head: there was one key and Jason took it from the safe: there were two keys and Sylvester had managed to get hold of the key Jason had taken; there were three keys all along: one taken by Jason and lost and two in Mr. Harries' possession. One key, two keys, three keys.

I sat in that chair for some time. Then I remembered the flowers; I went into the kitchen where I had left them on the draining-board; they were already beginning to droop. I took a vase and put them in water.

Then I looked sharply round, for I heard a voice I knew. Martin was leaning in the kitchen doorway, looking just as he had when we were first married, dressed for work in his black suit, his clerical collar, his hair soft, brown and wavy, his gentle face smiling at me. 'There,' he said, 'It was obvious all along what had happened.'

I shook my head slightly and said, 'But I got it all wrong.'

'No,' he said firmly, 'You *found* him.'

There was no-one in the doorway. The colours of the flowers swam before my eyes. I said, 'Oh Martin, I miss you, I miss you so much.'

A short while later I drew the curtains in the sitting-room, and sat down with a mug of tea. Jason Bell was dead and nothing would bring him back to life. It was time I stopped being a detective. If it was murder, there is a verse in the New Testament: Romans chapter twelve verse nineteen: 'Vengeance is mine, says the Lord, I will repay.'

XXVI

I am now in my late fifties. I have the house Martin and I bought together, and with the death-in-service payment I received when he died, and my own money, earned and inherited, I have enough to live on. It won't be long before I can draw my eight-years' teaching pension and my eleven years' Church of England pension.

I did not take up Bishop Robert's suggestion of becoming associate priest at Bereston but I do take services there from time to time when the Local Priest is away, as I do in many of the Tarnswell Churches.

The fourteen years that I was married to Martin will always be the happiest of my life. We cannot hold on to people forever.   We are always moving forward, and we will never, as they say, reach the next chapter of the book that is our life, if we keep on re-reading the last one.

So now it's time to think about the future.